Death's Touch

Erme Lander

Cover image – Panagiotis Lampridis

ISBN 978-1-8382157-8-1

More frog than princess, Erme Lander lives in Gloucestershire with her two children and a mad cat.

Other books by Erme Lander

The Vampire –

A Dark Inheritance
A Dark Infection

The Medici Chronicles –

The Lion of Ackbarr
Blood Lore
Medici of Ackbarr
Blood Debt
Warlord of Ackbarr

Lord of Dust

Death's Touch

Short stories

Sasha
Willow

Table of Contents

Prologue

A shiver ran through the registrar as her hand cramped. She looked up at the shadow crossing the room, not sure what she was expecting to see and blinked. Certainly not the child standing at the door, his presence a mute testimony to the war-torn country and one of the many that had filed through the office this afternoon. The registrar sighed and rubbed her eyes. She was overtired, it had been a long day and she hated dealing with the children. With no energy left to be compassionate, she said shortly, “Come in.”

He carefully sat where he was told, his head tilted and legs swinging. She placed him at about ten years old despite his eyes being too old for his face and the odd way he had of listening with his adult manners. Trauma had many manifestations and while she wasn’t qualified to deal with them, she’d seen plenty. She asked her questions judiciously, receiving little more than a quick nod or shake of a head to the few he answered silently.

She stood him in front of the wall with the marks showing feet and inches and thought of the clean bed in the tiny room she had to herself as she took a polaroid. Guilty pleasures, so different from the crowded dormitory these children would share. Knowing the faces of the children would file through her mind before sleep, depriving her of the comfort she craved made her voice curter. Under the weight of her self-imposed guilt, she ignored the slightly different cast to his skin under the dirt - he was a child and how he’d got here was none of her business. Her job was to process and get him into the system that could help.

The registrar caught a glance of amusement and frowned, those eyes were making her uncomfortable. The forms were filled in quickly and she watched the boy leave to see the nurse with a sigh. Sanitised from the vermin he most likely had, weighed and measured, then maybe someone would recognise him from the photo she'd taken. She doubted it and turned the page over ready to deal with the next innocent casualty of the conflict.

No one claimed him. He had no name, no papers and no voice. Eventually they gave him both papers and a name, placing him in one of the many overcrowded orphanages. No one was surprised when he sank out of sight, children disappeared from these places all the time. In fact, by the time they'd discovered the orphanage governor, dead in his office, no one noticed that the boy's papers had gone missing either.

Chapter 1

Tomas sat back in the dark corner of the bar room, drew on his cigarette and idly wondered if she would allow him to get lung cancer. Custom was fast paced tonight, with many people coming and going. The careless wealth these people had, and with no knowledge of hurting or hunger. The twist of their bodies, even the older generations could move easily, touching and laughing. He knew the sharp pain of hunger and had seen too many incapacitated by life's unfairness. His eyes slid through the crowd, picking out people's gestures, the laughter and shouts washing over him. The cigarette slowly burnt into ash as he drew on it.

He was the outsider here, the cast of his features proclaiming it to all and sundry and wiping away the grime and dirt of his day job did little. Still, most were polite enough to pretend not to notice unless they had reason to. Avoiding the reflection in the mirror above the bar, he watched the clientele, hearing the swirl and clink of the ice cubes in his whiskey above the music playing in the background. He snorted to himself - ice cubes - the amount he'd paid and he had ice not whiskey stones. He'd have to drink fast and not savour it as he wanted to in this trendy place. Maybe that was the idea, the cash tills had been busy all evening and most here appeared to be more worried about not being seen than a lack of money.

As for himself, he'd be lying to himself if he hadn't come back here to see the woman. Tomas absently flicked the ash into the saucer provided and ground the stub out. Last night he'd caught a glimpse of her, the flash of dark eyes and those cheekbones, they couldn't belong to anyone else. The delight as she'd met his gaze and then confusion at her reaction. He'd flicked his own eyes away in a stranger's politeness and continued walking, his heart thudding furiously and cursing over being so obviously leaving.

The cubes rattled through the amber liquid, he'd positioned himself where he could see the door tonight, if she came in then he'd see her. Irritation ran through him at his fantasies, she didn't know him, she'd just think he was a stalker after a chance encounter and in a way she'd be right. Tomas snorted again and tossed back the remains of the whiskey, briefly considered ordering another one and decided his wage packet wouldn't cope. He'd come back next week, another glimpse would be enough to bolster him, to reassure him that the world was turning as it should be and then he'd leave her to her life.

He stood and began the long weave to the door, sliding past couples with an absent intent. No one would look at him and remember his face, he was just another man with his skin suggesting a winter pallor in the olive complexion. He could be from anywhere, dark eyed, dark haired and he preferred it that way.

A woman backed into him, laughing. Not expecting it, Tomas automatically twisted to catch her arm, his hands ready before he realised she wasn't a threat. He saw the thrill run through her as she glanced up - she'd remember him tonight. He smiled and courteously let go of her elbow, the rough skin of his fingers catching her sleeve before she had the chance to ask him to join them. She wasn't the one he wanted.

The thin bile of disappointment rose, he was an idiot. He could sit in this bar for the next month and she might not come, the meeting was a happy coincidence of someone who looked like her. How many people were on this island? Sooner or later those same features would crop up. Tomas shouldered his way through harder, ignoring the muttering about his rudeness. He'd grab a beer from the local shop and drink it in his room, he had an early start and work tomorrow. A smile over the prosaicness of his life flitted and then vanished as he saw her near the entrance to the toilets.

"Hephzibah."

The name dropped unconsciously from his lips, the name he'd given her so many years before. Her eyes swung through the crowd searching for someone and passed over him without recognition. Tomas moved closer, ignoring the shoving of the crowd, could it really be someone who looked that much like her? With so many people in this world, someone had to have that same mystical combination of genes. Her head turned again and she saw him, her eyes widened slightly and she dropped her gaze to look at her phone.

Tomas left her to her unconscious distancing from him - it was enough. He walked to the door at peace with himself, he could leave now, his heart full at the sight. He paused to allow someone to push in front of him, hearing the hiss of heavy rain coming from outside. A shrug pulled his collar up. With no proper coat to keep it out, he'd be soaked by the time he was home. He smiled and he'd be kept warm by the memory of seeing her.

A small group of people were sorting themselves against the weather outside, umbrellas were going up, shoulders hunching in anticipation. He paused just outside the entrance under the canopy and was jostled by a man desperate to get inside. The rain was bouncing off the pavements, Tomas swore and jerked away from the wet shoulder brushing against him.

A ping and the man collapsed. There was a split second where he wondered what was happening and the sharp warning jerked him upright to let the man fall. He was dead and death he was used to. Tomas flung himself backwards into the doorway and the safety of the building as bullets sprayed through the people only preparing themselves for the mild horrors of a winter's evening in London. For a moment there was only the sound of the bullets hitting flesh and the walls around them, then the soft mutter of something happening before the realisation of hurt, and the confusion over the appearance of the deep red blue spray of arterial blood.

These people had no idea, instincts he'd not had to use for years resurfaced – he had to get to safety. Too aware of his own soft flesh, he ducked under shoulder height of those still standing, pushing past and hoping to hide. A brief flicker of guilt at others dying was subsumed by the rage of someone shooting here in a civilised country. He'd come here to be a number amongst many, to get away from battles and war. Where were those fucking bullets coming from?

Tomas shoved his way past the last person, pulling the stranger in with him through the door. It was chaos out there, bodies strewn in a widening pool of black puddles in the neon light. There was a ripple of horror as those inside saw the injured and heard the bullets ripping into and through the open door. He almost heard the collective indrawn breath before the screams began. Tomas feigned a stagger and the man he was using as a shield automatically extended an arm to help him. His mind was working overtime, it would be ten minutes at least before the police could get here, he had to find a way out. The panic started inside, the noise rising. People with phones to their ears frantically called numbers, others looked for another way out while yet more people, detached from the scene held up their phones to record it.

The crowd began to turn into a shifting pushing mass and Tomas wondered about his instinctive reaction to get under cover, being trapped in here could be equally dangerous. A woman stumbled into him and he pulled her upright, trying to make eye contact with those around him. The music that people had been dancing to only minutes before now drowned under the rising hubbub. He hoped it wouldn't take long for the police to get here, they'd cordon off the area and make it safe. There were some benefits of living in civilisation despite the restrictions someone in his position had. That gun man would be found or at least spooked off. Tomas wondered who he'd been aiming at and grunted as he was shoved hard against the bar.

He saw a flash of long dark hair and remembered his hoped for paramour. The woman was holding onto others in the shifting mass, her eyes wide and darting everywhere. Her gaze met his and they widened further. That made him react, he'd get her out and then he'd have an excuse to talk to her. These places always had a back passage, the slowly thinning crowd and heave of people in one direction proved it. Tomas knew this woman wasn't who he wanted her to be but he could have a pleasant hour or two pretending. Who knew what might happen after that hour with a grateful woman and a shared traumatic experience? He shoved himself away from the bar where he'd been trapped and began to work his way towards her.

The crowd resisted, tables had been moved and chairs dropped on the floor, waiting to be tripped over. Everyone was trying to get out of the back now. A large space had opened up between them and the door, only a few brave souls had stayed to try and help those still moving.

Not Tomas, that warning he'd had was enough and he had no wish to find out if the gunman was still there. He shifted, forcing his body between people, using the bulk he'd developed from the manual labour he did during the day. The flash of blue lights came outside, the police had arrived – good. He was almost close enough to touch her now, the crowd carrying them both and they were close to funnelling into the narrow passageway that led to safety. Her head turned and she noticed how close he was, her lips parting. So close, he ignored the shouts of protest and concentrated on reaching the woman in front of him. Her dark eyes flicked to the side, another horror in them and the warning nearly knocked him off his feet this time.

Tomas swore, his head twisting to see who was around, his hands open and ready. Where the fuck was it coming from now? In this crowd all he could see were panicking faces, intent on getting away. They were almost at the door, he caught a glimpse of the games room beyond and the crowd shoving towards the exit.

As though in a dream, he felt the regard. He turned, trying to stay on his feet and saw a large man pushing towards him, his face calm and his eyes locked on Tomas' face. For a moment Tomas stopped in disbelief, why would he be a target? He was one person in a crowd. Then woman forgotten, he attempted to push his way through faster, trying to look in both directions at once, the hair rising on the back of his neck. He had to get into the next room where he'd have space to move. He could feel the adrenalin shifting up a gear, making him more aware of the crowd, the music still playing a ridiculous counterpoint to the panic and the burning eyes fixed on his back.

A gun shot close by, deafening in the small space. Screams started again and the crowd heaved apart. The doorway to the next room was within touching distance and beyond it the crowd had loosened, everyone moving faster towards the exit corridor. Three of them tried to get through it at once and they jammed, Tomas swearing at the other two men stopping him getting to safety. They ignored him, flailing. The crowd pushed against them all, packing them tighter together and he considered his options. He was trapped with them, unable to move, he had to get out.

Tomas swore and a sick feeling spread through him at the thought of the permanent solution to the problem of him getting through the door. His hands were on the man struggling against him, seeing the white of his eyes and knew it would be easy even with so many witnesses around. He braced himself, reaching within when another loud explosion echoed nearby. Tomas jerked away as the man against him collapsed and his hands automatically tried to hold him upright despite their previous intentions.

They recoiled at the warmth of blood spilling. The dead weight fell sideways and released the jam, Tomas and the other man almost falling with the body. He twisted to pull himself through and looked back to see an open circle between him and the stranger who had been staring at him. Tomas' eyes dropped to see the gun and time slowed as the man barrelled his way towards him.

People scattered in the dimly lit room, the lights low over the pool tables. Tomas shifted across the doorway and moved to the side to get out of the stranger's line of sight and force him closer. Everything fled his mind apart from the figure, nothing else mattered. He made himself breathe, he only needed to grab this man's arm as he came close. He launched himself forwards, turning sideways to create less of a target, his hand outstretched. Just one touch, he reached inside at the same time, waiting for the right moment. The man's eyes widened and Tomas swore he could see fear. The hand holding the gun raised slowly, too slowly and Tomas grinned, a rictus. The man would be too late - they both knew that fact despite Tomas not knowing how. His hand closed around the stranger's wrist and he waited for the impact.

Tomas' jaw dropped as nothing happened. The arm beneath his hand was still rising, he'd not put any weight behind his block, he'd not expected to have to. The fear in the other man's eyes changed to triumph and Tomas heard the explosion at close quarters.

He was in shock as he felt a white hot line raze itself across his stomach. For a moment he staggered and then rage filled him at the injury. He'd dealt with worse than this, she'd left him injured badly before now, his suffering wasn't anything she concerned herself with. His grip on the stranger's wrist tightened as his training kicked in. He twisted the wrist to the side, lashing out with his other hand and stomped down with a foot.

Warmth flooded across his belly as his stomach muscles shrieked in protest. He couldn't look down to assess the damage, everything he had was concentrating on the struggle. Details flashed, the smell of sweat, the grunts as they both shoved against each other, banging into the pool tables. Hazel eyes met his as Tomas forced the gun down. They had moved away from the crowd, further into the room, the shouts from other people unimportant while they fought. Life and death, nothing else mattered.

The man twisted and brought a knee up, Tomas shifted too slowly and the line of pain concentrated into a ball of fire. His hands released to cradle his stomach, falling away to crouch helplessly. Sickness spread through him with the agony and he saw the man raise the gun again, a smile on his face.

The man's lips moved silently, "Favoured no more. Your god has abandoned you."

Tomas stared, unable to move, watching the finger tighten on the trigger, the dark muzzle of the gun was an abyss he was destined to fall into forever. The gun went off, loud in the enclosed space and the screams seemed far away. Darkness gathered and he waited for the expected pain, hoping she would be merciful. He fell into her warmth, a smile forming on his lips and knew no more.

Chapter 2

He stood in the clearing, the moonlight bright through the branches of the trees. He was thirteen again and terrified. A step forward revealed the pool at the base of the standing stone. In the half-light it looked as though it could swallow him whole and send him down to the centre of the earth. It reminded him of the dark muzzle of a gun rising and he groaned in remembered pain. He was dead, she'd brought him here for a final judgement, had his years of servitude not been enough?

Part of him railed against this replaying of an ancient scene, the older wiser part telling him that nothing was worth what he would have to promise. His thirteen year old self didn't care, his world was crumbling and it was the only way to make it right again.

Sanctity stole through the grove and crept into his bones, erasing the resentment he felt towards her. His younger self fell to his knees, pressing his face into the damp grass. "Please…"

"Tomislav?" The voice was from far away.

Without thinking, he raised his head and stared into the black pool, that other part of him knowing he would regret this choice for eternity. He was helpless, his limbs shrinking into those of a child. The lip of the pool was at his fingertips, there was nothing to be seen apart from the reflection of the full moon in all its glory. The surface was still and bending further, he saw the reflection of the child he had been, the tangle of dark hair and the determination in his eyes despite the terror.

He reached out to touch the surface and the voice came again, calling him, demanding his attention. Tomas overbalanced and fell into the pool, shattering the moon into a thousand shimmering fragments. The darkness engulfed him, wrapping itself around his limbs and stopping him from fighting his way free. Trapped by his promise for years - he couldn't breathe, his limbs becoming heavy. In a massive struggle he fought for breath, opening his mouth he drove the air into his lungs. Pain lanced through his stomach and he choked, the obstruction sliding out of the way and he breathed for himself.

Tomas slowly became aware of the beep of a machine, the still air on his face and crisp sheets holding him down. The moon became a small light in the corner of the room, reflecting off the white walls in the dark. He concentrated on breathing, a new found delight. He lay on his side, trapped by the sheets and became aware of the smell of disinfectant, the footsteps echoing in a corridor outside and the cry of someone in pain. His muddled brain slowly pieced all the puzzle together, he wasn't dead, he was in a hospital.

Light flashed further into the room as a door opened and more noise intruded. A shadowed figure bustled around him, tucking the sheets in tighter, "You were fighting the anaesthetic Mr Horvat, we had to take your tube out early. However you should be fine now, we've monitored you for several hours and we're taking you onto the main ward for the rest of the night."

Monitored for several hours? How much time had passed without him knowing about it? There was a pull as the sticky tabs of tracers were taken off him and the beeping stopped, the silence un-nerving. He slowly remembered the man raising the gun at him and the pain in his stomach as he'd been kicked. Somehow he'd been taken here, he'd survived.

"You've a drip in your left arm, please don't pull it out." The nurse's voice was business-like. "You had surgery to sort out that wound to your stomach, you're lucky to be alive." The door opened again and stayed open this time. He squinted as she raised her voice, answering a murmured question. "Yes please, ward nine has space."

He fought the need to cling onto the bed as it jerked and began moving. His eyes focussed on the tube feeding into the back of his hand. Helpless, he was tugged into the bright corridor unable to do more than watch the walls moving. She'd not taken him then, the knowledge that he was alive gave him no pleasure. After what had felt like miles, Tomas was brought into a large darkened room, the mutterings and snoring of other patients splitting the quiet. The nurse checked him over but he was already falling asleep.

Tomas woke with the announcement of breakfast ringing in his ears and the slow movements of the sick getting up. He was still lying on his side, tucked tightly in. It took a few minutes for him to remember where he was and what had happened before he began fighting the constraining bedclothes.

He was attached to a drip in the back of one hand and he felt the brush of another tube further down. He winced at the thought of the catheter and almost chuckled - he'd survived a gunshot wound slicing across his belly, a catheter should be nothing. The partitioning curtains were drawn back as Tomas finally managed to pull himself into a sitting position. He submitted himself to the checks and withdrawal of tubes, agreeing to the various instructions given by the nurse to make her go away. Everything felt bruised and out of sorts and the last thing he wanted to do was be here.

The morning dragged with the slow consumption of food he didn't really want, the longed for cigarette that was forbidden and the knowledge that if he wanted to, he could sort his healing a lot faster than lying in this hospital. The simple fantasy of sitting in a proper chair with a glass of whiskey and smoke filling his lungs consumed him.

About half way through the morning a male nurse came into the ward with a wheelchair, caught his eye and came towards him.

Wanting to stop the expected questions about his health, Tomas asked, "When can I leave?"

The nurse laughed, "You've a few days yet, enjoy them. In the meantime, we've a visitor for you."

Tomas hissed to himself, being ill wasn't something he enjoyed and frankly, he felt vulnerable here without any escape route planned. He sat in the wheelchair offered with bad grace and was taken into a private room on the next floor. A large man sat there, not in uniform but Tomas could tell a man who was used to being in command. His internal swearing increased, he disliked calling attention to himself and the law was that twice over.

"Please don't tire Mr Horvat out inspector. Tomislav, if you'd like to leave please ring the bell." The nurse placed a staff button on the table beside him and left.

"Mr Tomislav Horvat? Can I just go through a few questions about last night?"

The bloody man had a notepad, held casually in his left hand, a pen at the ready in the other. Tomas deliberately roughened his accent and smiled self-deprecatingly, "You're welcome to, but I don't remember much, I fainted after I was kicked."

Age had its uses, he'd played the charming foreigner so many times it was second nature to him. Men heard the accent and assumed he was ignorant of so many things, women were attracted to it and gave him far more leeway than they would normally. Add his skills at watching people to work out their intentions and it was a lethal combination. He had a few blind spots, but he was generally aware of them and acted accordingly.

The other man ducked his head, chuckling. "I'm not surprised, that was one hell of an injury you took there." He looked impressed, "And you kept going. Luckily for you, one of our men got trigger happy and distracted your attacker. My name's Stef Ludwick by the way. Here's my I.D." Tomas peered at the card offered and outwardly nodded at the confirmation. Stef's rank was higher than he'd thought, he ran through all his forged papers in his mind's eye, everything should be fine, he was sure he'd not forgotten anything.

"I heard the shot, I thought he'd shot me."

"No, you wouldn't be here if that had happened." Stef continued with a smile, "So, you are working here as a labourer on one of the building sites? You're employed by the local agency." He stopped at Tomas' bitten off swear word and waited.

"I haven't rung them to say I won't be in." He raised his hands as though looking, "I don't know where my phone is…" A good distraction, the industrious foreigner worrying about his job.

The other man obliged, "I'm sure we can ring them to let them know you're in hospital. It's good to have employment, will you be going for citizenship?"

Tomas shook his head, not taken in by the rough and ready mannerisms. Shrewd eyes were behind them and no doubt the mind would take in everything as well.

He shrugged, "I doubt it, I like to travel and meet new people. I will move on by next summer."

The detective's head was nodding in time. "Being able to work anywhere is one of the good things about Europe ehh? So, you are from the Croatian border?"

He'd done his homework, Tomas' unease increased. "Yes, I grew up during the conflicts. Maybe that is why I like meeting new people, I have found most like the same things in life. It's reassuring."

"It is, it is. Unfortunately there are always a few bad apples in every pot and that's the same everywhere too. Last night, what happened?" The man's eyes were on him, watching intently.

"I finished my drink and was just going out. I stopped in the doorway because it was raining, got shoved by a man trying to get in and then heard the gunshots. I ran back inside with everyone else." He didn't mention those who had died. "People started panicking, I thought I could get out the back and followed the crowd and then I was attacked." Tomas shrugged the best he could.

"Any idea why he attacked you? Did you recognise him at all?"

"You have seen him more than I did. I am no one special, do you think he had a grudge against foreigners?"

"We don't know. Did you see who was shooting outside?"

"No, it was raining hard, I wanted to get home. What happened to the man who injured me? Will he go on trial, do I need to give evidence?" The last thing he wanted to do.

"You're safe from that." The inspector sighed at his look, "Maybe I shouldn't say this but he died."

"Died?"

Stef said slowly, "As I said, one of our men got trigger happy."

"He was shot by the police? You killed him?" He couldn't believe that the police here would shoot a man dead. Even with only injuring him, the paperwork would be horrendous as well as the media attention.

"Not quite. He was alive when we got to him and he got brought back here, the same as you. Then he developed sepsis. The doctors said they'd never seen anything move so fast, nothing they did stopped it." He paused, looking a little green, "And then when they tried putting him on life support, the machine failed. Just like that."

Those words from the man and the look in his eyes when he'd grabbed his wrist, "Favoured no more." Something shot through his stomach that was nothing to do with his injury - that man had known what he was. In all the years he'd walked the earth, he'd never knowingly come across anyone the same as him and now he was dead. Hope and confusion crashed through him in equal parts.

"Are you okay?"

"I'm starting to hurt." It wasn't a lie, Tomas shifted and winced at the dull pain inserting itself into his consciousness.

"Can I speak to you tomorrow? See if you've remembered anything else?" Stef asked it politely, knowing that as far as he was concerned, Tomas wasn't going anywhere with his injury. Tomas agreed, with the personal intentions of not hanging around for him or anyone else. The inspector shook his hand and Tomas pressed the button to be taken back.

Tomas submitted to the doctor's prodding when he got back to his bed, the satisfaction over his wound and took the pain killers given which made him drowsy again. The slow morning passed into lunchtime and beyond. A flurry of movement caught his eye and he levered himself up into a sitting position, not wanting to be seen looking so vulnerable and wondered if he could draw the curtains to give himself more privacy. He watched the visitors in lethargic curiosity, it was mostly older women and he remembered it was the middle of the working week. The exception was a man of about his own age, his clothes dusty from building sites, a newspaper under his arm and his body language suggesting he'd rather be anywhere but in a hospital. His eyes passed over Tomas and he turned to walk away. A nurse flicked a look at his work scuffed clothes and disapproved.

Tomas grinned, the inspector must have rung his work. He called out, "Luc."

The man turned, "Tomas." He flinched at the looks and lowered his voice, "I didn't recognise you."

He slapped some chocolates on the bed and perched on the plastic visitor's chair. More used to the rough and ready shouting across building sites, he indicated the chocolates and said, "I drew the short straw, Sarah in the office was going to come but we thought that was the last thing you needed." Tomas had to stop himself from chuckling. Sarah had a thing for accents and it was a standing joke on the worksite that if anything was needed then they'd send the man in with the thickest accent to charm her.

Luc continued, "You look dreadful. Why the fu…" He paused, too aware of his surroundings, "Why did you tackle a man with a gun?" He stared in fascination at Tomas' midriff.

"It happened." Tomas shrugged with a wry smile. He liked Luc, he was simple and uncomplicated. "I'll ring the agency to let them know I'm not coming back for a bit."

Luc snorted and waved the paper, "I think everyone knows you're not coming back for a bit. Have you seen the newspapers? You're a local hero!"

Tomas swore to himself and took the newspaper offered, scanning it quickly. Five people had been pronounced dead at the scene, seven more with injuries and he'd been feted with taking down one of the gun men before the police had shot him. The other was still at large and Tomas ignored the rumblings of an enquiry about the shooting. Two photos were shown, one of the bar during happier times and the other was of him. He recognised it as his photo from the employment agency, normally he faded in with the rest of the cheap labourers but they'd not lost time in proclaiming that they knew him when he'd done something right. The feeling of unease increased, there wouldn't be many with names similar to his here.

He handed it back and shifted down gingerly, thinking quickly. "Look, can you do me a favour? I've got no clothes here, at least nothing to wear that's not covered in my insides. Can you take my keys and pick some up from my apartment?"

Luc blinked, Tomas could see him imagining the state of his clothes and he shook his head, "I'll have to go this evening, I've got to go back to work this afternoon."

"Thanks. This evening will be fine, I'd appreciate you doing it." Tomas swore to himself, he had no chance of getting out without clean clothes, he'd have to wait until later on. He directed Luc to take the keys from the plastic bag in his drawer, relieved that the nurse had told him they'd separated clothes and personal items and bagged up anything covered in blood.

Luc left a residue of building site on the chair after he'd left and Tomas stared at it. Yesterday he'd been working on the same site, dreaming about seeing the woman in the bar. Today he was in hospital. He absently accepted the food given on a tray by the orderly despite having little appetite and then winced as he shuffled down the bed to lie flat afterwards. Those eyes, widening as they'd spotted him. Yawning, he imagined her held against him, the hands sliding down his body and fell into pleasant dreams.

His dreams became deeper and darker and the woman's eyes changed, becoming colder. His hands no longer held her, they beseeched, raised in supplication. The moon reflected in a small pond, perfectly round and perfectly centred. The dark shape of the standing stone to the side. Her shadow turned away and desperation filled him - was he no longer favoured?

The memory of the dead man's words stung despite the fact that he'd never felt his gifts were such. The moon glanced off a cheek, he saw the lips curve into a smile and then he was alone by the pool. His hands fell to his side, filled with exhaustion and he waited for the darkness of sleep to engulf him. Instead the warning slowly rose instead, no words but the state of fear and the urging to do something.

Chapter 3

Tomas jerked his head up, cold with sweat and fully awake. He stifled his grunt at the sharp pain – he'd forgotten his abdominals had been cut.

Where was the danger coming from? He looked around, nothing had changed in the ward that he could tell. The grey afternoon light coming in through the windows was swiftly turning into a winter's dusk. He shivered, he was helpless here. On his elbows, he shuffled slowly back up the bed. There was more of a bustle around, people moving down the aisle between the beds. He looked at the clock on the wall, he'd slept for several hours - it must be the evening visiting time. A nurse came round, checked his notes and gave him some more pain killers. Tomas swallowed them in relief.

When would Luc be coming back? Surely he would make it tonight, he needed those clothes to get out of here. It was six o'clock, that would give Luc the chance to get to his apartment and back here when work had finished. He worried over the warning he'd had, she seldom interfered unless there was a reason and his thoughts stopped as he saw the woman in the aisle.

It was her. She was wearing the same leather jacket, her dark hair framing the olive skin, everything speckled with rain drops. Her eyes met his and she flushed slightly, dropping her gaze. As though firming her resolve, she walked up to his bed and asked, "Mr Horvat?"

He felt like he was in a dream, this woman who had the shape of one he'd lusted after so many years ago was actually talking to him. He managed, "Yes?"

"I saw your name in the paper, I wanted to thank you. You stopped that madman." Her words came out in a rush and she waved a newspaper. Tomas shrugged, not quite sure what to say - he'd defended himself, nothing else. He forced himself to keep his eyes away from the open collar of her shirt, it showed a strip of flesh leading down to somewhere that he didn't want to imagine his fingers following. At least not with her in front of him. "I noticed you at the bar the evening before, I was going to speak to you last night."

There was a note of desperation at his silence. He swore inside, he was a bore and she must be thinking she was a fool. Awkwardly he said, "Well, if we were at the bar then I would ask your name and if I could buy you a drink."

Relief filled her face. "I would say I am Perrette and it would depend on the conversation that went with the drink."

Perrette - not the name he expected of this woman who held the face of someone he had dreamed about for so long. Tomas shook himself mentally, this was a real live woman not a collection of longings. He forced a smile, "In that case I would ask if I could sit down in order to ply you with amusing tales you wouldn't believe." He waved a hand at the plastic chair next to his bed, he noticed someone had wiped the seat before she perched on the edge.

She smiled back before ducking her head slightly away. "I never believe the tales of men in bars Mr Horvat."

"Tomas, please." He felt inane. Despite his years, his experience of women was limited to chance encounters and short affairs. Life in war zones had a habit of restricting those opportunities and his vows didn't help with anything more permanent. He briefly wondered if there had been any children from the women over the years and mentally shook his head, concentrating on the woman in front of him.

"So, my drink would be a red wine, what would you have?" Perrette appeared not to have noticed his distraction.

"A whisky." Tomas let his accent deepen, "And once we had found a table, I would say I am a shady character with an unbelievable past and one who will not stay for long, although delighted to enjoy your company if and while it could be shared." He let his eyes speak more than his words and saw her flush despite the rising mischief in her own.

The short silence was pleasant and he almost believed that he might have a chance for a dalliance. Any sweetness in his life was there to be treasured, doubly so from a woman who looked like this.

"Mr Horvat, you have another visitor." He nearly swore at the nurse bringing the unwelcome interruption.

Perrette immediately jumped up, "I must leave you to your family."

"I do not have any family." He reached out a hand to stop her, he didn't want to lose the precious moments they'd had.

"I will come back tomorrow."

"What if I'm not here?" He was only half teasing, he didn't like being in this place. Even being at his apartment would be better.

"But…" She stopped her protest and carried on their daft story, smiling, "Then I will see you in the bar, at eight."

"In the bar." He'd wait in that bar for a week if he had to. Tomas watched her leave, the sway of her hips and thought about that gap in her shirt where a man's fingers could slide down to undo the buttons…

“Tomas.” Luc’s voice raised a few eyebrows at the volume. “I can’t believe you are already charming the women. Have you persuaded her that you need extra nursing?” He dropped a bag on the bed, chuckling at his own joke. Tomas winced as his backside followed, jolted out of a pleasant daydream and wondered if Perrette had heard. “Your landlady saw me, she said to tell you that several friends had already been asking for you.”

Friends? He didn’t have any friends who would go to his flat, all his acquaintances were from work. Was this what the warning was for? He forced the panic down, he had to get out of here. He had clothes now and there were more people around he could use as cover. He took the keys from Luc, making out he was tired. Luc cheerfully accepted both his excuses and his thanks and left.

Visiting time wasn’t over yet, he still had a chance. Tomas stood slowly and found the reception desk. “I would like to leave.”

“You are Mr..?”

“Horvat.”

She looked at his notes, “Mr Horvat, I don’t have a prescription for your pain killers and your doctor hasn’t authorised you ready to leave our care. Do you have anyone to look after you at home?” At his blink, she nodded. “What happens if you need help?”

A surge of anger ran through him, they weren’t going to let him out easily so he was going to have to do this the hard way. He ducked his head, pretending to agree. “My apologies, I didn’t think.” He smiled sheepishly at her, allowing a warmth to run through.

She smiled back, “Do you need a hand to get back to your bed?”

He shook his head. “Will you ask a doctor to come around in the morning? I would like to speak to him about arrangements.”

"Of course." His embarrassed shrug was rewarded by her smiling again, no doubt she thought him impatient and she'd be right. He took his time shuffling back to the ward, hunching slightly and conscious of his stomach aching through the pain killers.

Tomas closed the curtains around his bed and started dressing as quickly as he could. The trousers proved difficult, he hadn't realised how much he used his stomach muscles and he was sweating by the time he'd finished and dizzy from the exertion. His stained clothing went into the bag with his documents. He peeped out of a gap and waited until a woman stood to leave, gathering her two children. The staff hadn't seen him dressed up to this point, all he had to do was get off this floor and then he'd have a chance.

He closed his eyes and asked for help, he only needed five minutes. He'd give her a reward later, he promised. For moment he thought she was ignoring him and he pleaded harder, he needed to get out of here. With a glacial creeping, the pain eased and he stood upright. He'd done this before and knew he'd pay for it unless he could find a way to heal shortly but first he had to get out of here. Tomas slung the bag over his shoulder and walked swiftly out of the ward, following the woman leaving her husband. The children argued good naturedly and he smiled at them, playing along with being in their family unit while they passed the reception desk.

It worked, the nurse didn't even glance in his direction. The stairs were close by, he pulled open the door and all but ran down them. Tomas was counting the seconds off as he ran, this trick had helped at other times, enabling him to move when others had thought him incapacitated. Two flights down – he walked out of the stairwell and into the next corridor.

The pain hit him as he stopped in front of the lift, leaving him nearly doubled over despite the painkillers. No alarm had been raised yet and he tried to walk normally as the lift doors opened. The bag wasn't heavy, just awkward. He could feel sweat beginning to drip off his face and he reached the lift by sheer willpower. The jolt of the lift going down made him clench his teeth. He made himself remember, she'd be waiting for him in that bar. Tomas no longer cared that she wasn't the woman he'd wanted. He was going to make sure they'd enjoy at least one night before he left.

In a haze of pain he walked through the reception area, trying to stay upright and normal in the crowd of people. He wove through them slowly, everyone here was concentrating on their own world of misery. He caught the eye of a man sat in one of the plastic chairs and forcibly pulled his gaze away, refusing to show any weakness. His figure stayed in Tomas' mind, a tall thin man with a heavily shaven chin. It made him walk faster, his lips tight, he didn't want anyone to remember him.

The cold air hit as he walked outside, it was raining lightly, the neon lights sparkling in the puddles. The bustle of people moving through the front doors, the flash of blue from the ambulances queuing to disgorge their passengers. He breathed shallowly, trying not to aggravate his stomach. Not quite believing that he'd got out without a fuss, he slung the rucksack across his shoulder and hissed. He needed to get this wound sorted.

Tomas looked around and asked nicely inside, hating himself. "Please," he whispered as he walked through the car park towards the safety of the anonymous streets.

He could feel his stomach protesting, nausea and black spots threatening in his vision, all he needed was one last favour that would benefit her as much as him. A sick feeling spread that had nothing to do with his wound. The potential wasted so he could live, he was a coward and always had been. A tug directed him, weaker than it had before, almost a whisper. Tomas frowned, she wasn't usually this circumspect. She was the one who normally pushed him, demanding her due. The benefits to him were merely a carrot she dangled, to get him to do as she wanted.

Not far, he paused to allow himself to breathe, knowing that if he left it much longer then he'd be found flat on his face in the middle of the road. So far his escape had been a success, there'd been no outcry, no pursuit. He had another short window of time to get to his flat and pick up the few belongings he couldn't do without. He would be recorded as leaving on the CCTV but that would be it. He followed the gentle tug, aware of the unsavoury area so close to the hospital.

The narrow alley was dark and uninviting even in this modern city. He stepped carefully over the piles of rubbish, if he fell over here then he'd be helpless until someone discovered him. There would be undesirables around, the dross no city wanted to admit they had. It helped to think of them like that, rather than admit they were unfortunates like himself, dealing with the cards life had dealt them. He snorted, although his had been a choice, albeit one without knowledge of the actual consequences.

A shadow in the dark night, someone covered up as far as possible to hide from the cold. He jingled his pocket, pretending to find loose change and reached out to grasp the hand open in supplication. A touch, a sigh and the grip loosened with no worry for the cold any more. Tomas straightened fully for the first time since the hospital, adjusted his bag with ease and walked out of the alley, no longer needing to mind his stomach.

He'd collect his few personal belongings from his apartment, give in his notice at the employment agency and stay in a guesthouse for a few nights. The agency would be easy to disentangle himself from. Tomas refused to think that he was separating himself from what he'd just done, that would be discovered later. The only string attaching him to this life was the woman, he paused, and was she enough to make him stay? He consulted his phone, looking for the nearest bus routes and walked with a purpose, watching the road while his thoughts jostled for attention.

Any kind of publicity would make him easier to spot in this digital world, pictures could be plastered over the internet and sent across the world in seconds. In times past no one used to care, friends were all you needed to speak up for you, a voice of respectability so easy to come by if you were socially minded. Now papers, passports and cards were all hoops to jump through unless you were willing to live on the margins of society and he had done that in times past. He could see in the future there would be more times like that and he sighed, he liked his few comforts chiselled away from the rock of society.

A bus was waiting further up the road. He ran, waving for it to wait and jumped on, paying for his ticket. Perrette – he folded his arms tightly and stared hard at the back of the seat in front of him, avoiding the dark reflections in the windows. She'd been open to the idea of something, why else would she have looked for him? They both might have fun if they were like minded, a night or two in a guesthouse and then he could slide away. She'd be upset no doubt, when he disappeared but he had warned her of that and they were both adults.

The miles crept by and Tomas stood to get off, nodding to the driver, confident of his anonymity in this part of the city. He knew there'd be a few extra grey hairs that hadn't been there before in the dark shock of hair, if he was lucky Perrette wouldn't notice. His steps brought him closer to the block of flats he lived in and he imagined her on top of him, his hands sliding up her smooth thighs to pull them closer together and smiled to himself. There'd be plenty of time to think about that when he'd packed and enjoy the logical conclusion to his fantasies.

Tomas tapped the number into the keypad to get in the main door, a smile still on his face. The lift smelt of piss as it always had, his flat was one of many piled high in this part of London. Here he was a faceless person in a tower of similar working bodies for sale at low prices. They were there so those richer had cleaners and nannies, gardeners and nurses.

His fingers touched his door as he began to insert the key and he stopped. Not quite a warning, he'd felt a breath of something not right. He slid his rucksack off his shoulder and gently placed it onto the floor beside him. His eyes flicked around, muscles tensing. Just as well his stomach had healed, he'd be in no fit state for anything otherwise. Tomas placed an ear against the door and listened, filtering out the music from the flat opposite and the crying child downstairs.

What was he expecting to hear? Luc had mentioned his landlady saying there'd been people asking about him. He silently muttered something rude, his landlady was nosy, always wanting to come in and check on the condition of the place. He deliberately kept it immaculate to wind her up. Had she allowed someone in to wait for him or was she using the opportunity to look around for herself?

He stayed, frozen in place, the blood pounding through his ears for minutes stretching across an eternity. A soft noise as though someone brushed against a piece of furniture, a creak of floorboards - it could be from another flat or from his own. He had to get in there to pack the few possessions he had and there were a number of items he couldn't replace. He inserted his key and braced himself.

Tomas turned it and flung himself into the room, moving swiftly sideways. Shock flitted across the man's face who was standing in the middle of his living room and he ran for the door. Anger surged through Tomas - first the insult of bullets being sprayed across him in the street, then a total stranger attempting to kill him and now this man in his flat. His anger streaked down, his arm reaching out. The man dodged, stumbling backwards, fear widening his eyes. He banged into the table and Tomas used the moment to grab for his arm. There was a thump and his body fell to the floor.

Panting in the aftermath, Tomas reached through the doorway to drag his rucksack inside and slammed it shut. He stared at the mess in his flat, nothing had been left unturned. This couldn't have been done before Luc had been inside, he would have said. He found himself stepping over the body to begin shutting drawers out of habit and stopped.

"Run…"

The command was a whisper, the echo of thunder in the distance after the lightening. Tomas agreed and didn't stop to think any further, he went through his few possessions quickly shoving items into a larger rucksack. The flat was rented, he'd take most of the money out of the account later. If the rent kcpt coming then his landlady wouldn't complain until there was a smell and let's face it, this man was an intruder. Who would complain about him going missing?

He considered his options, he was going to have to move, to disappear faster than he'd wanted to. The woman would have to be dropped. He could feel himself shutting that part of himself down out of habit. Someone appeared to know about him and he didn't know what or how much. A new name, a whole new identity was needed. Maybe even a different country, he swore, building another personality wasn't easy these days.

Tomas pulled on different clothing, more suited to an older man. They were a little baggy around the waist and shoulders but that would be sorted shortly. It was time for his current persona to disappear, thankfully he had another ready to take on, he just needed to get to his documents. The man he saw in the mirror now had more than just a few silver hairs, he brushed his fingers through absently, pulled open a drawer and picked out a heavy knife from underneath the spare clothing. The handle was smooth and familiar despite him rarely needing to use it. He tucked it into his rucksack, knowing that its presence had probably been noticed by the now dead man.

He pulled a hoody on and left the hood up to hide the difference in his hair. It looked a little strange on a man of his age but he didn't care, it wouldn't be for long. One last thing - he opened the airing cupboard and reached behind the door to pick at a bubble in the paintwork. It peeled off in a strip of painted tape with a key attached and he sighed in relief that it hadn't been found.

Tomas stepped over the body, noting the heavy duty boots and muscular build, this wasn't an average cat burglar taking advantage of an empty flat and he wondered if he was linked to the man in the bar. He took one last glance around, his now ex-landlady would throw a fit, all her fears about letting to an immigrant founded despite his paying on time and keeping things tidy for the last few years. He shrugged and tossed the front door key onto the mat inside the door, pulling it tightly closed as he left.

It wasn't a long walk to the next building and it was hushed in the quiet evening, most of the workers gone home. Tomas showed his ID, gave the key to the man on duty and was given an envelope in return. Renting a po box wasn't ideal but it was the best he could do these days. He called the agency, citing the need to stay in hospital and recover at home as his reasons for not being at work for a while. With luck they'd forget about him quickly, there were many waiting to work in his place. He changed the sim card in his phone for the one from the envelope and dropped the old one into a bin as he passed.

The rain had reduced to a gusty squall, he settled the rucksack and closed his eyes, asking the question. This time he had no qualms, he needed to disappear. There were no shortages of the homeless despite the advertising campaigns trying to get them off the streets. Away from the CCTV cameras and into the back alleys where few would normally walk they would be plentiful. This time her answer came without hesitation and he walked with a purpose. Given a choice of them or him, it would be him every time, his cowardice demanded it almost more than she did.

He came out of the alleyways having stuffed the hoody into his rucksack and did up the sports jacket, it was a little thin for this time of year but he'd be under cover soon. The belt holding his trousers up was pinching, he undid it with a sigh and headed towards the underground station close by. This time he used the paperwork in the envelope, he flipped through and found the debit card, it had enough on it to last several weeks if he was careful. He'd have plenty of time to sort the rest of his money and transfer it over. The platform was quiet, only a few people waited with him.

The journey on the underground to the main station was uneventful and the train he was after would be leaving soon. He relaxed, confident in his new persona. The platforms were busier here, but still not overly so. No threats were apparent as the train he wanted was announced, this was the main train out, it only stopped at certain stations before it finished for the night. It would be a taxi drive and then a long walk after he'd got off.

There were about ten minutes before the train departed, Tomas decided to get a coffee and something to eat before he got on. He'd want to sleep if possible and not mess around trying to find the buffet carriage. He caught his reflection as he stepped up to the window of one of the shops, an older man with iron grey hair and deeper lines in his face returned his gaze. Tomas smiled, he was still recognisable as the man he had been but who would expect someone to age at least ten years in an evening?

He came out with his nose buried in the cardboard cup and juggling a plastic bag with his rucksack. He'd slide off to his hidey hole and stay there while he decided where to go next. This aspect of him wasn't too old to work manually, he could feel the power still in his older muscles and his mindset wouldn't be too fixed either. That was good, so often the body dictated the mind if he wasn't careful. The testosterone of youth getting him into scrapes barely thought through and the rigidity of old age. Tomas shuddered, maintenance had become important to him in more ways than one.

There were still a number of people milling around the platform, Tomas had been about to move out of the crowd and get on the train when he saw two figures come running out of the entrance in front, they stopped in dismay at the train and the people boarding. The woman ran ahead a little and paused, her eyes searching the carriages and Tomas swore to himself - it was Perrette.

Chapter 4

He stepped back into the shelter of the shop front and watched as Perrette waved her hands at the man, gesturing at the train. The announcement sounded that it would be leaving and he watched to see what they'd do. There was no way that he could get on without being seen and even with his extra years disguising him, he was reluctant to try. The man had his back to Tomas, he couldn't see his face but he could see Perrette, she ran her hands through her hair, winding it around her fingers in frustration. The man had his hands on his hips as the doors locked closed and Tomas gritted his teeth, watching the train slowly moving off.

He watched them move away towards the entrance and gave them as much time to leave as he could. What was Perrette doing here? She'd given the impression that she'd wanted to get to know him for far more prosaic reasons. Tomas swore, he was too edgy and it was one of too many coincidences.

Tomas flicked through his phone for coach times and left the platform in a vile mood, he'd been looking forward to dozing in comfort and a coach wasn't the same. He pulled his collar up, knowing it wasn't much of a disguise and hailed a taxi. He brooded all the way to the station at Victoria, that man in his flat, his landlady saying that people had been around and Perrette turning up at the station. He'd been lucky with the last one, two seconds later than they would have seen him. He stifled his inner swearing as they pulled in, maintaining his deception of being an older, respectable man and paid the taxi driver.

The taxi shot off for his next fare and Tomas straightened, taking in the station. There was a coach in the next thirty minutes, just enough time to buy a ticket and scan his surroundings. He frowned, there were a number of uniformed figures talking to passengers waiting at the stops. More coincidences, he twitched, no longer feeling quite so secure. Tomas shifted his rucksack, he didn't want to have it searched and the knife found. That would be an excuse to bring him in regardless of whether they suspected him of anything else.

He no longer felt he had any other options, he had to get out of here. Tomas strode into the open space feeling a distinct chill and bought his ticket, walking towards the waiting area indicated as though he had other thoughts on his mind. He stopped politely at the officer barring his way.

"Can I see some identification and your ticket please sir?"

"Of course." Tomas nodded and gave the officer his new passport. He stood almost at attention, an upright member of the community, grey haired and dignified with his years. Another man joined them in plain clothes and was casually shown the passport. Tomas swore behind his façade, it was the inspector from yesterday.

Stef glanced at the passport and up at Tomas's face. His eyes widened and then narrowed. He waved his own identification, asking, "Going anywhere nice sir?"

"Yes, I am seeing a friend in the countryside officer."

"Not by train?"

"I missed it unfortunately." He spread his hands, looking for sympathy.

Stef hesitated, searching his face. Tomas could tell he was looking for some clue to link him back to the man he'd seen in hospital. "I'm sorry to ask this sir, but we are looking for a man who was injured." Tomas could tell Stef thought that he'd stripped hair dye out somehow to disguise himself. “Would you mind obliging us by showing us your stomach? We are very concerned for him as he left hospital with a considerable wound.”

Tomas showed the confusion benefitting an older man asked to bare his midriff on a cold winter’s evening and then turned slightly to shield the other people from the sight. He undid the last few buttons of his shirt and showed six inches of healthy hairy belly. The inspector’s face was completely baffled, he’d been sure he’d correctly identified Tomas despite the changes.

“May I go now sir? I need to catch my coach.”

Defeated, Stef gave the passport back. “Yes, please do. Accept my apologies for the intrusion.” Tomas nodded and walked away, buttoning the shirt and tucking himself in - a pillar of respectability on the outside and full of a vicious satisfaction on the inside.

The coach arrived and Tomas got on, watching the police stopping the occasional man with dark hair and asking for identification. Hunted, the need to hide somewhere rose and he was pleased when they pulled away without any further problems. The streetlights faded into the flash of motorway and he dosed, intermittently staring out into the night. The coach was half full and he twitched every time anyone went past him to use the toilet. The drone of the engine soothed him and he fell into a fugue, finding himself reaching out a hand in his dreams.

“My lady, I have honoured you well these last few days.” The words were unspoken, what else could he give her apart from his devotion? “I am your servant…”

A crescent moon appeared behind his own face, turning to become the face of a dark eyed woman, her cheek pale against his olive one, the colour leeched out in the cold night. The briefest of brushes pressed to his cheek, her lips compressed into a slight smile and the phantom dissipated. Tomas sighed, these small moments settled him back into what he was, despite his hatred of what she made him do. The pain he felt was worth it to worship her. His eyelids closed and he slept until the coach pulled into the next stop.

Perrette's form haunted his sleep, or rather someone who'd looked like her. Her slender body under his hands, her clothes morphing into those of another similar woman from centuries ago. She'd been married to a travelling merchant who was respectable and far older than her. Their whispered courtship had happened under the trees, hidden from view on the outskirts of the small town where he'd been working as a labourer. The feelings he'd had stirred him even now, he'd been sure she'd felt the same way. Their coupling had been passionate and he'd often wondered if he'd left her pregnant in the years afterwards. There'd been something sad in her face that had drawn him, a timeless patience…

Tomas groaned as he woke, he'd fallen asleep in an awkward position. He was the wrong age for this sort of stuff and a touch young enough to believe that he could get away with it until he found he couldn't. The driver was calling the name of his stop as he pulled the coach into the car park. The other passengers equally bleary, watched as muttering, he collected his rucksack from the luggage rack and stomped down the aisle.

He stood to one side as the coach drove away. The small village was quiet, it wasn't quite closing time for the pubs yet. The large car park was lined with houses and a playground on one side. Tomas shivered, the wind was biting here, he needed a warmer jacket. He also needed food and other essentials more urgently and those he could get if the small shop was open otherwise he'd have to cope with the tinned goods he'd squirrelled away.

Little appeared to have changed in the last ten years or so since he'd been here. Tomas didn't like to come too often, there was no point in making a trail to a hidey hole. The tiny local shop was thankfully still open, its aisles cramped with goods. He grunted his thanks at the teenager serving him, grateful that he'd not been forced to converse and reveal his accent.

The local taxi dropped him off at the junction to a housing estate. The driver had been equally surly, wanting to get back for the pubs closing. Tomas blinked at the size of the estate, there'd been nothing but fields and farm buildings here the last time. He hoped the local youth hadn't regarded his private land as a challenge and realised he needed to keep an eye on planning applications near all his bolt holes.

The night was chilly, Tomas watched the taxi drive away and blew on his hands. He riffled through his bag and pulled out the hoody, no longer caring what he looked like. Stamping his feet, he walked up a footpath through fields, his torch catching glimpses of the black humps of cows browsing. His muscles warmed up, unstiffening with the exercise and he stopped several times to look at the map, swearing at the unfamiliarity in the dark. Maybe he should have found a bed and breakfast to sleep at and yet he couldn't stop the nagging feeling that he needed to be somewhere safe and the bunker was the safest place he could think of.

At last he climbed over the half tumbled down wall and was into the woods that his current persona owned. They were wild and full of brambles, the paths had clearly been used by the locals as they weren't too overgrown but nothing appeared out of place. It wasn't far now and the distance alone from the lanes winding through this countryside would protect him. He walked next to a tiny steep valley with a stream running through it and smiled at the noise of the water trickling over the rocks.

Tomas concentrated, this next part wasn't easy, especially as he'd not been here for several years and the dark made everything harder. He peered in the limited light of his torch, the edge was here somewhere. Too close, swear words burst out of him as he slipped and slithered down the bank. He lurched out of the stream in disgust, rubbing his backside and picking his feet out of the cold water. The streambed was a mass of mud, clogging his shoes and threatening to soak his feet. Tomas flicked the beam of light both ways, unsure which way he needed to go. He stomped off alongside the stream, choosing the direction at random and relaxed as he saw the hook in the valley where the stream made a turn.

Tomas crouched to check that the race was still in place for the turbine, he'd need that for the battery. He shifted a large stone to divert part of the stream to run down into what looked like a hole and heard the soft whirr of the wheel turning in the hidden chute. He was taking a chance starting the turbine up without checking it but it was cold and late and he wanted light. From the water race he turned his back and slowly climbed the slope, muttering a little at the stiffness of his older body and its new bruises.

He took a moment to orientate himself to find the tree stump a short way from the stream. Tomas shoved at it, noticing how it had rotted more since he'd last been here it and it refused to move. Swearing, he leant a foot against it and slipped sideways, leaving a trail of mud as the top half moved to show a handle in the hollow depths. He was more tired than he'd realised. Tucking the torch under his chin, Tomas spread his legs, braced himself and heaved.

Slowly the handle began to move up and he saw another movement in front of him in the torchlight, a trapdoor shifting under the years of leaf litter. Tomas wedged a branch through the handle to keep it from moving down again and ran over to the trapdoor, shoving another stick in to keep it open. In the morning he'd clear all this, at the moment he just wanted his bed. With the trapdoor exposed, he allowed the handle to sink back and pulled the stump back into place.

An aluminium ladder led down through the concrete tunnel. Tomas swung the rucksack off his back to fit through and swore as he found it coated in mud. He slid down inside, knowing once the door was shut then the leaf mould would cover any signs of it being there. There were a few inches of water at the bottom of the ladder, obviously the drains had blocked somewhere, a penalty of living underground. The switch for the battery was in the main section, one click and the bare light bulb flickered into life. It was damp down here and austere but he'd be safe.

Tomas sighed, he could get used to this again if he had to. Blankets were in the metal cupboard, damp from age but usable, he winced at the smell and then smiled at how fastidious he'd become over a few short years. He pulled a few out to toss them onto the bunk at the side. It creaked as he rolled himself into it, he'd decide what he was doing next in the morning.

Chapter 5

Tomas spent the next few days sorting the bunker or rather, sorting out both of them. He'd originally started in less curious times by bringing the pieces of curved corrugated iron up the track and camping out in the summer weather. Covered in mud, he'd nearly finished digging the length one afternoon when his spade had hit something with a clang.

With the deliberately younger body chosen for its strength, he'd carried on in curiosity, digging far past his natural point of stoppage. Youth had its drawbacks as well as its advantages. Tired and hungry, he'd gazed at the curved pitted wall of corrugated iron, similar to the ones he'd been using to hold back his own walls. Obviously someone else had decided at an earlier point that this site was suitable for a similar purpose. He'd had to go and buy a hacksaw and cut through the wall. There'd been no way to dig around it to fit the rest of his bunker in and he couldn't not know what was behind the wall, stubbornness being another disadvantage of being young.

Now in the present, the two bunkers joined in a dogleg, the original was bigger than his and set higher causing any water to drain into his part. It had partially collapsed at some point early on in its existence, the fall of earth covering what would have been the entrance and it looked as though the back exit had been filled in deliberately. After the initial blast of fetid air, he'd discovered the abandoned remains of supplies left on bunks and in cupboards and the half covered pile of arsenal in the earth slide.

He'd installed a piece of now warped chipboard into the props to stop everything from sliding further into the bunker. It appeared safe enough, he had no doubt she'd give him adequate warning if they went off, she'd done that before. The chipboard also hid the bones of someone unfortunate enough not to have the same early warning system from casual view, it was probably the reason why the place had been abandoned. He'd wondered if there'd been a family left waiting for him, if they'd been told or if the others who had dug this place had slunk back in guilty silence. Years too late to do anything about it, he'd left them where they were, they were only bones.

He inspected the pile in the light of the bare bulb, it hadn't slipped any further despite the slow weep of damp collecting in the lower levels of his bunker - it had just rusted a lot more and the chipboard needed to be replaced soon. He'd done some investigation since the dawn of the internet and discovered the munitions pile should be fine unless there was something to set it off. A gleam of white showed in the black earth.

Tomas smiled at the emerging skull and said, "Still here and not talking? Well, it's a bit of company at least." His smile deepened at his whimsy and he left to walk down to the village.

He was aware of his crumpled clothes as he walked, the village had changed more than he'd realised in the last few years. There were many more retired people and more holiday makers in the picturesque place that had housed a farming community. The pubs catered for tourists, the shops the same. He'd been lucky to get what he'd needed when he'd arrived, in the slow creep to winter everything would soon be closing down.

There was a single bus to and from the nearest town and that was it, everyone else drove. He'd felt years ago that the bunker was a perfect place to hide out for several months or years if needed, now he wasn't so sure. Years ago, no one had cared about how you dressed and he could hide his olive complexion amongst the sun blackened farmers. It was also too early in the day, in the height of tourist season he'd have been able to mix in with the crowds without notice, now he was sticking out. He waited for the bus, watching the few people straggling out of the single coach to stare at the picturesque buildings and sighed, wishing for the busy streets of the city.

Tomas got off the returning bus late that afternoon, his rucksack full. The laptop he'd bought was snugged into his back, he'd be able to transfer his funds across this evening and find out what was going on properly in the outside world on a decent screen. Then it would be getting off this island and into the continent, disappear for a few years and pop up somewhere else with one of his other identities. She'd sort his age out in her own unnatural way, he mentally flicked through some of the passports he had hidden and sighed at the difficulties of civilisation these days.

"Tomislav!" The name was called out good naturedly, making him jump and blink. His mouth formed a question and he cursed at the moment of inattention. Tomas made himself to keep walking while glancing casually around. A man was stood in one of the doorways, a smile on his face. Tomas' own was now carefully blank.

The inspector fell into step with him, raising his hand as though to clap him on the shoulder and dropped it before he made contact. "I am Stef Ludwick. We met at the coach station." Tomas damn well knew who he was and wasn't happy about it. He tensed when Stef reached into the pocket inside his jacket and relaxed a little when he only brought out his I.D. "Would you like to have coffee and talk it over?"

"I remember the coach station but I don't know you sir." He tried not to let the recognition come into his eyes and acted confused while covering his racing brain. He'd never had anyone pick up on his identity so quickly after he'd changed it. "And Tomislav is not my name. Have I done something wrong officer?"

The other man was still looking friendly although Tomas was sure it was for the benefit of the people around them. "Let's not mess about shall we? You are Tomislav Horvat not the name you are hiding under now or at least you were. You were injured in London. Somehow you have managed to conceal your wound and disguise your age as well as having different identification. Shall we talk?" Tomas felt caught on the brink of a precipice, on the one hand he wanted to get as far away from this dangerous man as he could. On the other....

"I'm not sure what you are talking about officer, however if you are offering a coffee?" He had to know who this man was.

"Of course."

Stef led the way to one of the many tiny coffee shops and they sat down at the frilly table. The waitress took their order and left them staring at each other. Tomas studied the other man surreptitiously, he was about ten years younger than Tomas' current age, shorter and stockier. With brown hair and eyes, he would blend in nearly as much as Tomas himself. Tomas caught his glance, the other man was studying him in a similar way.

"I didn't think you actually existed."

Tomas frowned, "What are you talking about?"

Stef leant back as the waitress reappeared and put the coffee down. He stirred in milk and sugar, taking his time. "I started a project several years ago, a hobby you might say, every man should have one. I happened to be playing around with a facial recognition programme on a course I'd been sent on. If you'd have seen the two pictures side by side, no one would have thought anything of them but the programme brought up the man in them as identical."

"And?"

"They were fifty years apart." Stef's eyes were firmly on his coffee cup, stirring gently. "I showed them to the course instructor and he laughed it off as something to be aware of, we need to collect other evidence, facial recognition is simply a useful tool if used correctly."

"So you found its limitations." Tomas made himself take a sip from his own cup, he'd never thought of modern technology being used to uncover his past like this.

"No," Stef shook his head. "I looked for other photographs and found them, there aren't many but they are there and they are all from war zones. You are always in the background, never part of the main picture as it were. The software can model aging patterns from youth to old age as well as picking out identical faces, it's very accurate." He reached into his bag and brought out a folder. He laid out several photos and Tomas felt himself grow cold. They were all of him, at various points during the last seventy years.

Tomas picked one up, "This looks a little like me when I was a boy. Where was it taken?" He was bluffing, he knew precisely where it had been taken. The cold plastic chair and that woman so desperate to get away from the room full of ghosts. It was the easiest way to get identification these days, to enter a war zone as a child and get picked up by the local peace keepers. He was safe enough, even as a child, he knew he had no need to worry about being killed or injured – she would take care of him and would enjoy any ensuing sacrifice. He had several birth certificates tucked away for times like these, times where he needed to disappear.

"That is the man I spoke to you about, Tomislav Horvat as a child." Stef raised his eyes, pinning him and said softly, "His face fits yours on the software and it is one of the few clear photos I have. The rest of the paperwork disappeared, this polaroid had become separated by accident. I believe that the governor of that orphanage was found dead, roughly at the time the child disappeared. I also accessed the CCTV records from the coach station, your face fits as well my friend."

Tomas froze and tried to stop himself panicking and the rage inside rising. He'd never had anyone this close to him and especially not the law. He had to get out of here, dispose of this man and his dangerous speculations - one finger would be all he needed. He could feel the muscles in his forefinger wanting to move, a man suddenly falling over dead here with plenty of witnesses, it would be easy to protest his innocence… only it wouldn't. There would be an investigation and the police might become involved again. Either way, his current identity would be recorded, leading to a wider trail.

As though reading his mind, Stef said, "Please be aware that I have all my suspicions left in writing with a friend. Let's talk." He smiled without a trace of concern in his voice, "Please, no threats are needed."

"I am not threatening you." Tomas kept his voice even. Getting off this fucking island would be difficult if the police were looking for him, he'd have to resort to a shadier way. He'd never had this before, the world had been a much larger place for so long. Fifty miles were nothing, now you had to travel to a different country and even then you could be followed.

"What about the man in your apartment?"

"I don't know what you mean." He forced himself to smile and shake his head, to keep denying until he could get away.

Stef leant forwards, "The man you disturbed had put a camera in a corner of your apartment."

He'd thought there'd been something not quite right, so the man he'd killed had been a policeman not a casual burglar and they'd recorded what he'd done. Did they want an admission of guilt as well? Stef was only a few inches away, one brush of his finger would end any threat. He choked back his need to end this threat, he needed to find out what this person knew first, knock him off his guard. As though unconsciously realising his danger, Stef moved his hands away to clasp his coffee cup.

Tomas took a deep breath and repeated, "That wasn't me." He asked as though it was an afterthought, "A man in an apartment you say, a policeman would ask to come in with a warrant wouldn't he? Announce himself. Was there violence? Are you accusing me of doing something to this man?"

Stef winced and said slowly, "No, there wasn't a warrant for some reason. He was supposed to be collecting information only and was disturbed. What did you do to him? You touched him and he fell over, cardiac arrest. No wounds, nothing." His eyes narrowed and Tomas saw him clench his jaw against more words wanting to spill out.

Tomas relaxed a little, they couldn't use the evidence they had. They'd over reached themselves and the worst they could accuse him of would be not stopping to help this intruder – if they could prove he was Tomislav Horvat. "How would I know?"

"It recorded you dressing in the same clothes you were seen in at the coach station and putting a jacket in your bag that you wore later. You've not changed that much you know, only about ten years. Enough to throw off most people but not to someone who's spoken to or knows you. How did you do it?"

Tomas stared him out, his coffee growing cold. No evidence he reminded himself. "Officer, I don't know what you are talking about. I'm not the man you think I am."

"I think you are."

Thoughts were nothing, he couldn't prove it and he'd not done anything. A surge of elation filled Tomas, they'd have uniformed police here if they could, armed as well seeing as they now knew how dangerous he was. Not this single inspector who'd left notes with a friend. He nearly snorted to himself. No one would dare touch him in case they ended up in the same state as their colleague. He wondered briefly if the cause of death had been hushed up and cast it aside, they couldn't pin it on him. "You can't prove anything."

Stef narrowed his eyes, "I don't need to prove anything. If you are who I think you are then sooner or later the bodies will start to pile up around you."

If needs be he could go without changing his age for several years, the difference wouldn't be noticeable for a while. She wouldn't be happy but she could deal with that, his safety came first. He was almost vicious in his triumph. "That may be true of this man you're looking for." He sat easily, not giving an inch. "But it isn't me."

"Why did you react to me calling in the street then?"

"I grew up with a friend called Tomislav, we were very close." The lie came easily now.

The other man sighed and swept the photos into a pile. He scribbled a mobile number onto the back of the boy's photo and gave it to Tomas. "Here's my number, if you need me, call it."

"Why?"

"Because I'm a curious bastard, I hate a mystery I can't solve and it gives me an interest outside of work."

"You're a sad bastard." It came out without him thinking and he had to stop himself wincing, that was out of character.

"True." Stef gave a brief grin, not appearing to notice. "Call it if you need me." He got up and put some money on the table for the bill and left Tomas staring at his back and the cold cups of coffee.

Chapter 6

Tomas was left in turmoil, despite knowing Stef couldn't prove anything. Those photos, he could pin point every one of them. He turned over the one left to him with the phone number on the back and looked at the younger version of himself in curiosity. The dark eyes gazed back calmly. He rarely allowed himself to be that young unless he had a reason. Youth brought its own troublesome range of emotions, his life experience had only so much influence. He winced at some of the things he'd done while desperate to survive. Eventually it brought him back to the killing he despised so much. It was a cruel joke he'd had played on him, sometimes he wondered if it was deliberate on her part, forcing him to kill in the knowledge that he was taking something precious that he could never give back…

A rattle of cups and the waitress's shadow startled him, "Would you like a refill sir?"

He shook his head, "No, thank you."

She hesitated, "That's a nice photo sir, is it of you?"

"Yes." The answer didn't matter anymore. He stood and tucked it into his back pocket. Stef had left plenty and more for the undrunk cups, Tomas smiled at her and added some extra. He caught a glimpse of them in the window, the reflection showing an older man politely inclining his head and the younger woman smiling back at the generous tip.

The afternoon was wearing on into early evening. He needed to get back, sort out his money and decide what to do. Stef was nowhere in sight outside, not that he expected him to be. He hailed a taxi and told the driver to take him to the housing estate again. He'd used different routes over the past few days, now he no longer cared. Up to this point he'd always been able to stay under cover, never drawing the eye of the authorities. He wondered briefly if he could fake his own death and shook his head, that would bring its own problems of no I.D.

He muttered to himself as he walked through the fields, he'd had the chance to take it easy for a few years in a civilised country and he'd had that taken away by those gunmen. He clenched his fists, his anger lending a length to his stride, a few years was all he'd asked for. Some time to relax without looking over his shoulder for men with guns in war zones. He wondered if he should try America next and join the transient population there. There were so many people on the streets in those cities, he could lose himself easily.

Tomas sighed, first he had to deal with transferring money and then the problem of getting off this bastard island without anyone noticing. Both of his identities were suspect, why hadn't he sorted out a third? The answer came within a breath – because this was a civilised country and he shouldn't have needed it. He couldn't even go back to his previous identity because of his apparent age and the police's suspicions although he'd keep it running for the moment.

His angry strides brought him swiftly up to the tumbledown wall and he stopped, raising his head as though testing the air. Something had made his shoulders twitch, a sense sharpened by the years in war, both as hunter and hunted. He propped a foot up and fiddled with his shoelace, nothing but birdsong and the wind in the trees. No danger signs warning him from within, she was quiet. Just the feeling of being watched. He paused, pulling the air into his lungs like an older man taking a breather from walking too fast.

Still nothing. Was it Stef or one of Stef's friends? Was he really so desperate to get them all killed? It was a shame, he'd liked the other man despite his dangerous questions. His curiosity to know had pulled at Tomas, was it a need for a friendship deeper than the casual acquaintances he'd kept while working? He'd always stayed away from anything more, not wanting the inevitable grief of friends growing old.

Tomas sighed and hardened his heart, if anyone came through his hatch tonight then he was a dead man, and that included Stef. With a final glance, he climbed over the wall and into the wood, walking the long way round to his bunker. The feeling of being watched disappeared but he was still uneasy at the thought of more killing. Stef's words about the bodies piling up haunted him. Why couldn't she have chosen someone more suited to this, who actually enjoyed it. The darker thought rose that they would have been found, the bodies more noticeable. His sneaking ways had enabled them both to survive.

As a precaution once he'd climbed down, he wedged a piece of wood into the mechanism that enabled the hatch to lift from the outside – no one would be able to get in without him taking it out. His rucksack was dumped on the floor and he pulled out the laptop with the delight of a new toy filling him. Tomas had tried to keep up as much as he could with technology despite feeling like it moved bewilderingly fast at times. The information he could now access, it was a magical ability to be able to communicate with another person thousands of miles away, to read the words of people long dead. That had been a privilege of a few wealthy lords and monks for so many centuries. He remembered struggling through learning his first letters and the frustrations of making his hand form the words in a harsher age than this, his older mind knowing that it would be useful. He shook his head, no one appreciated what they had these days and chuckled, first world problems was a very apt saying.

Tomas was unable to do the task he was about to ask his new laptop to deal with, however he was very adept at making friends, especially on the shady side of life – he'd had years of experience at that. He switched the light off, the laptop would take more than the little generator could make while working otherwise and inserted the USB stick. He took a paraffin lamp out of the cupboard and winced at the smell as he lit it.

The screen lit up the rest of the room with pages of numbers scrolling and he left it with a smile. Instructions would be left to transfer money over several days, flicking it through many accounts, sometimes more than once into a trail that would take time to unravel. The man who had written this was dead now, from a drug overdose in a sunlit room. Such a waste of life, he'd been in his twenties…

He started frying some eggs on the little stove, cut some bread and smeared them with butter. This program would take a few hours and then he could start planning what to do next. He let his mind wander, he wanted somewhere with a place to cook, even a campfire would be better than this thing. Tomas flipped the eggs absently onto his bread and folded them into a sandwich. With his mouth full, he took a half empty bottle of whiskey out of a cupboard, time to relax. His phone dug into his backside and he wriggled it out with one hand while eating with the other. His wallet followed, landing beside the laptop with a thump and poured himself a whiskey.

The liquid burned as it went down, like the guilt he felt. So many wasted lives, how many of those he'd taken would have had the potential to become someone? He'd robbed them of the chance to find out, one of the reasons he tended to haunt conflict zones. It brought the worst out in people and therefore didn't fill him with quite so much guilt. Drinking also helped, it eased the memories of those moments when he took what wasn't his.

Tomas poured himself another and raised the glass with a wry salute to the unseen. Never too drunk, never drunk enough. He'd taken what they called psychedelic drugs once, never again. Leaving your mind wide open to your god was never a good idea, he could imagine even the most benign would take a power trip through your brain and his certainly wasn't.

An uneasy alliance existed between them, she could have demanded so much more from him, she knew his weaknesses and allowed him to rail at her. It was rare for her to demand her due - she didn't need to, the condition she'd placed on him had dealt with any such reluctance. The hum in the confined space and the drink lulled him, he needed to concentrate on his current problems not those of the past he could do nothing about. Tomas put the half empty glass back onto the table and shifted into a more comfortable position on the hard chair. He'd think better on a rested brain and sometimes she suggested ideas to him in more subtle ways.

Tomas woke with a jump, remembering his older body with a sigh and froze – something was wrong. The laptop was still flickering its numbers but there was a difference, the static feeling from the generator had stopped. He left his head resting on his chest and flicking his eyes around, noticed the laptop was running off battery. Was there a problem with the little water wheel? It could happen although it was generally a good system, another thing he'd learnt from others more capable than himself.

The paraffin lamp had dimmed, sending shadows into all the corners. Everything was still apart from the flickering numbers on the screen. It was seven thirty-two according to the computer, it would be dark outside and it was getting cold. What had woken him, had it been the electricity switching off or something else? Everything was still in place, no warning of danger from her and yet it felt as though she was holding herself tight inside, almost hiding… He tensed, she didn't want someone to know she was there, why?

Tomas remained seated despite his muscles beginning to scream, his eyes peering through the semi darkness, trying to see. He nearly jumped out of his skin at a flicker of movement and the soft thump. His nostrils flared, getting the oxygen he needed to move quickly. What had that noise been? Nothing else moved in the small space, nothing had fallen off the shelves or table. He slowly scanned the room, his skin prickling until his eyes rested on the mechanism and realised that the piece of wood had dropped out.

He looked carefully and found it on the floor, hidden in the shadows. He was sure he'd jammed it in there firmly, there'd been no movement of the mechanism that he'd been aware of. Tomas slowly stood, his own movements barely a whisper in the dim light. He reached up to the top of one of the cupboards and felt for the cold hard object lying hidden. His fingers found it as the sound of wind in the trees and a soft gust of cooler air hit him. He smiled, even if he'd not woken before, he'd certainly be aware of the hatch opening now, he'd lived dangerously for too many years.

The screen of the laptop went blank as he brushed his fingers against the keyboard and pulled the USB stick out. The first thing that loaded was an emergency wiping programme, nothing would be found. He tucked the stick into his back pocket, supressing the swearing he wanted to do at having to start it again later.

The ladder itself was hidden from view by a partition of iron, his feet were pantherlike as he crept towards it. Tomas composed himself, controlling his breathing, he'd have one chance at this. They'd likely have guns, he knew that he would in the same circumstances. Stef was going to have to understand the consequences of following him around. A soft murmur from above and he frowned, there was more than one person up there. The sound of steps on the rungs, whoever was coming down them was good, they barely made a sound. He counted the muffled scrape, the pause at the bottom and readied himself.

A slender figure slid through the gap in the door and stopped, her mouth dropping open, he knew she recognised him despite the age difference. His own shock was briefer, he pointed his gun at her and she waited, her hands slowly rising and watched him warily but without fear.

He indicated her to come inside with the gun, his other hand asking for silence. Perrette licked her lips, glancing up at the hatch. He grabbed for her wrist and this time she did show her fear – what was the difference? Did she know what he was? Tomas pulled her away from the ladder and into the middle of the room.

"They know you're here." Her voice was low and pitched for his ears only.

He was in no mood for being nice. "Explain."

"I'm supposed to persuade you to come out."

"And if I don't want to?"

"Then they'll kill you."

"That's easy then." Tomas held the gun up to her head, pulling her closer to him, his arm around her waist.

"It won't work. They don't care about me."

He didn't believe her, she was working with them but what was her connection to Stef? Tomas shook his head, that no longer mattered and considered his options, he'd never dug an escape hatch, never thought he would need one in this civilised country. So many little mistakes, one after another leading to being trapped here. He needed to get close to them, the chance to touch would even out any inequalities. Maybe he could use her, his arm tightened, pulling her closer. He'd not be able to get her up the ladder without letting go, his best bet was to stay here and somehow force them down. Indecision tore at him, they could starve him out or he'd be vulnerable as he came out of that pipe, his hands on the ladder.

"Why do they want me?" Tomas shook Perrette and jerked his head up as he heard more conversation outside and a shout. In the semidarkness he was hyperaware of everything, the muscles of her stomach under his hand, her quick breaths and the rustle of leaves outside. There were at least two men out there, he didn't stand a chance. Perrette opened her mouth to reply when they heard heavier footsteps on the ladder.

She had a catch in her voice, "They've got a semi-automatic. If you won't come out then they'll get you inside."

"Fuck that." The hairs rose on Tomas' neck, they meant business. He backed away looking for cover, he'd survived for far too long to have any intention of dying. A figure burst around the partition spraying bullets as Tomas dove behind the dubious safety of the chipboard panel, pulling Perrette with him. They landed heavily as the bullets pinged above their heads. The noise was incredible in the enclosed space, his ears popping. A warning shrieked through him. Perrette turned to say something, her mouth moving and they were both pulled into nothing as an explosion rocked the room.

Chapter 7

The explosion shook him and in that instant he turned to her, reaching out to grasp the insubstantial hand she offered. Warmth wrapped itself around him and he relaxed in the knowledge she would take him. Waiting for the peace of death, he spasmed as he was turned inside out and strained through a sieve, the very atoms of his being separated and put back together. It was like no agony he'd ever felt before, the scream building up inside and abruptly he was dumped into coolness.

Tomas panted, the pent up scream released with a wheeze and gradually he became aware of the woman in his arms. They were lying as they'd been thrown, an unconscious chivalry had pulled her across him so she would have been protected from the bullets. The silence hung hard around his ears and it took a while for him to realise it was actual silence rather than the deafness of the explosion.

He wasn't dead. Tomas raised his head to look around them. Instead of the dark bunker, there was a luminous mist around them. Trees and tufts of grass looked insubstantial in the half light. It wasn't even the woods above the bunker and it was the wrong time of day. Tomas frowned, this was no place he'd ever seen before. He flexed his fingers, the hand that had been holding the gun stung as though it had been ripped out.

Perrette muttered into his chest and pushed herself away. "Fuck it, that was the roughest transition I've had in a long time."

"What?" His voice was too loud in the quiet and she shushed him by raising a finger to his lips, the heat of her body close to his. She fitted seamlessly into the curve of his arm - the perfect place for a woman to be. He resisted the urge to draw her closer, not trusting her. She ignored him and sat up, apparently not affected by their closeness and he hauled himself up after her. He tried quieter, “Where the fuck are we?”

Perrette looked at him as though he were mad, “Didn’t you bring us through?”

“Through where?”

“To the Hall, although this isn’t a way marker I’ve been to before.” Her stare became incredulous and she said, “You mean you really don’t know where we are?”

“No.” Tomas put his hand out to grasp a tussock and pull himself onto his feet. His hand went straight through the grass and he fell flat on his face.

Perrette grabbed for him. “Shit this is worse than I thought, we’re in an area of low traffic. Look, even the marker’s sunk since we got here. We need to get away from here and onto the Corridor. That’s always stable.”

Tomas raised his face, attempting to contain the panic he felt at the spongy feel to the ground holding him up. The slender black stone that had been at their feet was now only about a foot hight. He carefully sat up again, tucking his feet underneath him to bring himself upright on the safe ground. Despite the earth being insubstantial, his trousers were getting damp.

“You know this place. Get us out of here.” He didn’t trust her, he reached out to take her wrist, his fingers overlapping it and ignored her flinch.

“I can’t believe you don’t know where we are.” Tomas said nothing, scanning the area. There was an eerie familiarity to this place but he couldn’t quite grasp why, he’d never been here before. She sighed, “Let’s stick to practicalities for the moment. The ground will be soggy here, if we don’t test every step then we’re likely to fall through. Our coming through will have solidified some of it temporarily but we need to move now."

Turning her back to the sinking stone, Perrette took a step forward. She immediately sank to her knees and Tomas hauled her back. His own feet began to sink with the additional weight.

"Fuck, we could do with a staff to probe this mess. Keep hold of me." She tapped her foot carefully in a circle around them, testing the ground and found a firmer spot. Perrette stretched and leant into it. Tomas braced himself the best he could, ready to support her. "Here, put your foot right beside mine."

Tomas lurched forwards and placed his inside hers. The ground was holding – just. They brought their other feet to rest on it and Perret began her probing again. This close he could smell the musk of her perfume and see the way her breasts strained against her shirt as she stretched out. He was aware of an emptiness behind them, a colder stream of air suggesting they shouldn't be in this place. There were skittering noises and the occasional screech in the background putting him on edge. He recognised none of the noises. He tried to look for danger while she tapped for the next solid footing.

"Don't bother, it won't help. Concentrate on what's under our feet."

There was little enough, the grass was soaking, the chill creeping into his bones. The only warmth came from his contact with Perrette. He was too aware of her in this strange landscape. She was too tall to tuck under his chin, forcing him to swing his head to one side as he stepped up to her again. The bones in her wrist were delicate under his hand, the creak of her soft leather jacket as she stretched to find the next firm spot was a tiny normality. Tomas shivered, his own coat was in the bunker and wondered again how they'd got to this place. He gritted his teeth when she motioned him to step up to her again and couldn't stop himself from glancing down at the gap in her shirt.

Perrette straightened and scowled as she noticed, "Can I help you?"

Annoyed at being caught he said drily, "I doubt it. One set of tits are very much like another and I've seen plenty thanks." Perrette snorted in return.

She ignored all the distractions around them and kept up her slow progress. The mist parted for a moment to show the black trunks of the winter trees and a trail leading through them. "Finally," she muttered.

Her steps became faster and even Tomas could feel the difference in the ground. He stepped beside her now until they were almost running and they reached the trees together. Perrette collapsed on the grass, pulling him down. Her wrist was still clamped in his hand. He released it, flexing his other hand absently.

"Your hand hurts?" She was almost smirking at him. "I thought you'd know the gods don't allow modern shit out here."

Hating his ignorance he asked, "What you do mean?"

She squinted at him, "It wouldn't have come through. I'm surprised you didn't get any broken fingers." Her manner was beginning to grate on him. He knew nothing about this place and it was a disadvantage he didn't need. She continued, "And I don't know why you didn't shoot Mark back at the bunker, you could have at least winged him when he was coming down the ladder."

"It's a deterrent isn't it? I don't need a gun at close range and it's something people understand."

"What do you mean?"

Embarrassment shot through the anger and he snarled, "It's not fucking loaded, okay?"

Her jaw dropped, “That’s why I wasn’t warned that you’d hurt me, you never intended hurt to begin with.”

Tomas grunted and stood, not wanting to talk about keeping an unloaded gun. He’d killed enough in his life, he didn’t have to explain his choices and especially not to her. “How do we get back?”

“We need to find another way marker. Don’t fancy trying to reach that one again.”

“Let’s get moving.” He could see a faint trail between the trees, “We follow this?” He began striding up the trail at her nod.

She started walking beside him but didn’t take the unspoken hint about not talking further. “We weren’t sure of you.”

He sighed at her insistence, “Sure of what?”

“If you were one of the gods’ favoured.” Tomas kept quiet, concentrating on the path and woods around them, they were like no other he’d seen before. He peered at the boles of the trees, the pattern of the bark was almost blurred in the half-light and he reached out to touch one.

“Don’t bother, they won’t be that distinct this far out. We kept expecting you to prove your status, most slip up at some point but you didn’t. It must be how you’ve survived so long without attracting notice.”

Survived - he almost snorted, the tree smooth and cold under his fingers. Years of war zones, moving from place to place so he didn’t have to keep adjusting his age and by default having to kill the ordinary people blamelessly living their lives. He pushed himself away and continued walking.

Perrette was persistent, “So, are you?”

“If that’s the way you want to put it, then yes, I am.” He’d never felt favoured in any way in all the years he’d lived. His condition was more a curse, forcing him to do her bidding.

“I knew you were.” He ignored the look on her face, concentrating on walking. The mist was thinning, the boles of the trucks clearer, drops of water hung from spider webs. “Who is your god?”

“Al-Kiron.” The reluctance he felt in saying her name, it jarred in a personal way as though he was stripping naked in front of a crowd. “You’re one of the gods’ favoured too?” All these years, he’d never met anyone like himself. To be confronted by this woman who had the body of someone he’d lusted after for so long and hear her say these words… He was having difficulties, this woman was very different from the woman of his dreams but no less attractive for it.

“My god is Dar.” She waited, obviously expecting a recognition.

“Never heard of him.”

They came out of the trail, the trees reaching out to arch over a paved road and Perrette put a hand up to stop him from stepping onto it. “This is the Corridor. Once we step onto it then others will know we are around.”

“Then we don’t step onto it?”

She huffed. “You saw where we came from, sometimes those soft areas get very close and I can’t guarantee we won’t fall through. It’s better to take the chance of being noticed and it’s faster on the Corridor.” Perrette turned and half closing her eyes, she pointed, “Dar’s that way, can you tell which way your god is?”

Now that Perrette had asked, Tomas knew. A clear straight line down the Corridor in the other direction, he could almost see the way… and she was hiding. Without thinking he said, “No.”

“Fair enough, we’ll go this way then.” She stepped onto the paved road and started walking. She didn’t believe him, he could tell.

“Tell me about this place, humour me.”

Perrette shrugged, "It's no secret to those who can get here. The structure of the Hall remains stable with the Corridor running centrally and with the glades to each side and…" She hesitated, "They move."

"Move?"

"Yes. It depends on the seasons, phases of the moons and how many worshippers they have in the physical world. They tend to cluster together and the glades are more substantial."

"What do you mean glades?"

She was becoming impatient with his lack of understanding, "Where the gods reside."

Tomas was getting more confused the more she said, "If they move, how do you know where they are?"

Perrette pointed at a large white stone covered in moss, a short way in front of them. "There, what do you feel about that?"

The stone was streaked in mould as well as the moss, there was an opening in the ever present trees and what might have been an overgrown track leading through. Tomas lengthened his stride to walk up to it and stared at the opening, unsure of what he should be noticing when a horror came over him.

Something was down that track, the grief beating its way out of the glade, coming to pluck at him with ghostly fingers. Al-Kiron was a lifetime away and he could feel how this god would promise him anything if only he would give her up. Surely it wouldn't be as bad… A hand pulled him into a stumble and he jerked himself upright. He blinked, the track was just a track again with a dirty white stone next to it.

"You really are new here aren't you?"

"What…"

"You need to use your own god as protection against the others here. We'd better move, that one's not been dead long and there's still an echo around. Not that there'd be anything left to see if we went into the glade apart from rubble."

Tomas collected himself, "What happened there?"

"As I said, it's the remains of a dead god."

So much he didn't know, the only hope he had was this woman he didn't trust. "Let's make a bargain, you get me out of here alive and I won't kill you." Tomas twisted his hand and captured her wrist. As before, he saw the tensing of her body - she knew what he could do.

She narrowed her eyes, "And when we get back you'll let me go?"

"Yes."

Perrette shrugged and her dismissal of her fear irritated him. "Done. We'll need to look for another way marker and get it to set us down where we want it to."

"Can you find one?"

"Yes but I don't think we'll find many this far out. I get the feeling we're a long way off the main part of the Corridor. Are you sure you don't know where Al-Kiron is?"

That had been asked too casually. "No. You wanted to go this way?" He turned in the direction she'd pointed and started walking. With her wrist clamped into his grip she didn't have much choice in not following.

"How did you manage to change your age? Was it to do with those shocks we felt?" Shocks? He had no idea what she was talking about She shook her head at his silence, "Someone invested a lot of power in you. You're the favoured of a god no one hears about, that no one's seen for centuries and yet here you are."

"And here I am," he repeated grimly striding on. Anything she didn't know was an advantage he had.

She let them walk on a bit further and asked, "Would you mind not holding my wrist like that? It's a little uncomfortable."

"I don't want you leaving me here."

"We made a bargain – remember?"

"True. Let's make sure you stick to it, shall we?"

Perrette laughed, it was an open sound and completely without malice. "You don't trust me and I don't blame you. Look, take my arm instead, I don't want to be this far down any more than you do." That rang true, Tomas hooked his arm through hers as she'd suggested.

"I can still stop you running."

"But you don't want to."

"I'd rather not."

"Not much of a priest for your god are you?"

"Maybe I've seen too much." He refused to speak further, glancing around. His nerves were jangling in this place, the distances didn't work properly. Things that appeared far away came closer too soon. Other landmarks faded into the distance from close up. Too many eyes watched from the trees, the tracks leading off into god knows where, he snorted - it was a good way of putting it. "Are all these gods dead here?"

"Maybe, maybe not. I'm not checking. This is uncharted territory for me, I normally stay in the area I know."

Tomas felt a shiver run through her and curbed his automatic impulse to draw her close. He didn't know this woman, she only wore the face of someone he'd known. She was a woman with a god, the same as him. He'd never realised that there were others like him, had always thought himself alone with his burden. Questions began to boil up, he wanted to know everything and came to an abrupt standstill as he saw the gleam of her eye watching him. He asked instead, "Any idea of how long to the next way marker?"

She shrugged, "Dar says it's not far but he's not one for details like distance."

Tomas suppressed a groan and kept walking. The paved path was smooth and gleamed slightly, the trees crowded close and faded away without warning. The moon rose full and bright over the trees and Tomas stared at it, wishing for some contact from his god. It was typical, this was the one place where he was supposed to be physically closer than he'd ever been before and she didn't want to know him. The line was still there, he could break away and run to her. The longing rose to find out what her marker would be like in this long stretch of horrifying gateways.

The standing stone by the pool he remembered had long gone. Centuries ago when he'd looked, he'd not been able to find it. Had it actually been there or had it been a figment of his imagination and a useful trigger for a desperate boy to pray at? That feeling he'd had in the grove, he'd never felt anything like it since. Tomas loosened his grip on Perrette's arm, he was going to find her, demand his dues, rail at her in person. She couldn't deny him here, couldn't…

Perrette grabbed his arm with her other hand. "Wait a minute," she hissed.

Something in her voice made Tomas freeze, his eyes darting about trying to spot the danger. The paved path was deserted and he glanced behind, nothing was there either. To each side, the woods crowded close and the breeze had freshened a little, stirring the branches but not the mist. In the middle distance, a pile of white stone flickered between different perspectives. He shook his head, trying to clear his mind, "What?"

"Listen." The chittering had increased from the bushes and a long drawn out hoot came from further away, echoing into the unknown. He focussed on the bushes close by.

"Which?" He barely breathed the word.

"That." The scratching coming from first one side and then the other. "They're behind us, we need to keep walking slowly. Don't run yet, they'll chase."

"What are they?" They walked, Tomas could feel his muscles tensing at the unknown threat.

"Cribbet. You'll see them soon enough although I hope we can get to the way marker first. I don't think it's is far now. See that tree? They only appear close to the way markers." The small tree was bent, swept in an invisible wind, the branches nodding. As they passed, it twisted upright, no longer showing the way. Tomas twitched away, shifting Perrette more to the centre of the path.

There was an edge to the laugh Perrette gave, "I forget how much this place takes to get used to it. You really are new here aren't you?"

He ignored her. Shadows darted in amongst the trees, low to the ground. They slid away as Tomas tried to fix his eyes on them. "Is that one of them?"

Perrette followed his nod, "Yes. They prefer to creep up from behind though. They know we can see them from the front and sides."

"A lot of predators are the same, I heard that villagers can foil tiger attacks by wearing masks on the back of their heads. The tigers think they're looking at them."

"I'm not sure I'd want to try that here. Cribbet aren't stupid and they don't always do the obvious." Tomas increased his pace, aware of her hand holding his arm tightly. The chittering had been joined by a rattling of scales, the rustling of the bushes becoming louder. “Fuck. They’re going to attack shortly, we need to stop now. Stand back to back, it confuses them.”

Tomas looked around, “We’ve no weapons.” He clenched his hands, knowing the creatures were far too big to get close to and he’d have to be within touching distance to have any effect.

“I’ve a knife.” She brought a dagger out from the inside of her jacket and she almost laughed at his look. “Next time you take a prisoner, remember to pat them down.”

Tomas stifled a swear word, “I’m pleased I didn’t. Still, from the size of those shadows that’s not going to do a great deal.”

“I’ve got a few tricks, Dar hasn’t left me completely helpless and others find me too useful not to let me defend myself.” Perrette smirked at him, “Don’t assume you’re the only one with an interesting talent.” Tomas’ questions were stopped by the creature running out onto the path.

Chapter 8

Tomas was experienced in conflict and had seen many horrors in his long life but he'd never confronted anything like this before. The shadows lurking in the woods had shown only the general size of the creature, not any details. He frantically scanned it, looking for vulnerabilities and found none as it rushed towards them, its scales rattling and huge jaws chittering at them.

Perrette muttered in his ear, "They'll let one attack first and then they'll all come. If we can down this one then they might decide we're too risky and we'll have a chance to run for the way marker."

It was enough to unfreeze his muscles, he glanced down at his hands. He had no chance, by the time he'd got close enough then those jaws would have him. Perrette had dropped into a crouch, her dagger ready to throw – was she mad? She'd leave them weaponless. Remembering her words about them attacking from behind he cast his eyes around them, checking for others and he missed her first throw.

The creature baulked, skittering to a stop making Tomas stare at the handle of the knife settled neatly into one of its many eye pits. He hesitated, too aware of not knowing how to kill this thing when another dagger whistled past and hit one of the pustules growing out of its armoured back. A thin wail scraped across his ear drums and something began pushing its way out of the skin, liquid seeping down the creature's back. He could feel his gorge rising at the blindly swaying miniature pulling itself free.

"Missed the little bastard."

Tomas tore his eyes away and stared at her. Perrette's face was concentrating, a mist appeared around her hand, solidifying into another dagger and she threw again. It settled into a seam in one of the scales. As he stared, he heard the rush of legs and turned to see another monstrosity rushing towards them, jaws clicking.

"It's not enough, they're all attacking!" Perrette's voice cracked in despair. She continued to throw her daggers at the one in front in desperation. It had collapsed onto three of its many legs and was starting to move in circles, unable to run away.

One was slightly ahead of the pack racing towards them, its long tail swinging the club at the end. Tomas could see the fine barbs all over the body that would make it impossible to grab. He'd have to put his hand on them and risk any injury. There were too many behind to touch and kill, they were going to die in this place.

"Fuck that." Tomas found his anger and flung his hand out at the onrushing monster.

A black flash sparked and sliced through the air, knocking it onto its back. Tomas almost squawked in surprise, watching as the pack pulled up, milling around in confusion. A vicious satisfaction cut through his amazement at killing the creature. "Got it."

Perrette turned round, mouth open in shock. "How did you… watch out for the babies, they…" She stopped as the pustules split and a putrid liquid spilled out, the tiny nightmares limp in death.

Tomas took a step towards the pack, not sure how he'd managed to kill it but determined to capitalise on his success. The rest of the creatures backed away into the woods, the chittering slowing and dispersing as they left their fallen comrades to their fate.

"We need to move while they're not sure of us." Perrette said it slowly, almost fascinated by the tightly curled up legs of the dead cribbet. She ignored her own maimed victim, still crawling in circles.

"What about that one?" Tomas waved at the injured creature, wondering if he could conjure the black flash of death again.

"Leave it, it'll buy us time." She shivered and wrapped her arms around herself, apparently unable to tear herself away from the scene.

"Come on." Tomas grabbed Perrette's arm and turned her to begin walking. Once physically distanced, she began to walk faster until she was almost running. Tomas could feel the quivering of her arm under his hand and suppressed the desire to wrap his arm around and hold her tightly. He kept a wary eye out, noting the cries and shadows in the woods while they moved.

"Here," Perrette had pulled herself together and stopped him at a small track, lined with black stones.

Tomas couldn't remember if the other one had been the same. "Are they still around?" He could still feel eyes on him.

"Probably, although they'll be more wary now. If they can completely surround us then yes, they'll attack. We need to get to the way marker before them. How did you do that?"

Tomas looked at his hand, it had never done anything like that before, he'd always had to touch. He shrugged casually, "Just a trick." He'd work it out later.

"Right," she snorted. He could tell she didn't believe him. "Let's keep moving."

As they moved away from the path and into the mist, Tomas could feel the change in the air and found himself walking on edge. "Are we going to start sinking again?"

"Maybe. We aren't near the well-used parts – remember? Hold onto me." She slid her fingers into his and gripped tightly. Her hand was small and he crushed the need to protect the owner. She was capable of looking after herself, more so here than he was. A shadow darted past them and his breathing became faster. Could he do that thing again? Chittering began all around them, growing louder as they walked.

"Are we nearly there? Can't we go faster than this?"

She shushed him, concentrating and began testing every footstep. "If we get this wrong then we'll fall through."

Remembering the soggy ground by the last pillar, Tomas didn't question where they'd fall through to. The noise became louder behind them, he constantly glanced back expecting to see the long humped bodies. Perrette's hand became slick in his and he absently unlocked their hands to wipe his on his trousers. A shape scuttled into sight, the scales clattering and he saw the rest rushing to outflank them.

"We need to move!" Tomas pushed her forwards into a run as it charged them. He whirled, palm out and the black streak flashed out to impale the monster.

Perrette's shriek made him spin back, frantically looking for the threat and found her on her knees, grasping at tussocks as she attempted to drag herself out of the hole. Tomas pulled her out, scooped her up and ran. This older body still had stamina although he wished for the younger testosterone-fuelled one of youth. He sank to his ankles in soggy ground and kept going, barely touching before leaping again.

The pack was behind them, scales rattling as they charged. Tomas couldn't tell how far they had to go, if they lost their footing then they'd be overwhelmed and his new found skill wouldn't make any difference. He could feel himself tiring, Perrette was becoming heavier but with no time to put her down, he kept going.

With his lungs burning, he saw the mist opening out in front of them, the slender black pillar was a knife in the night. More shadows came out of the mists to the sides, they weren't going to make it and Tomas bellowed his rage. He flung Perrette at the marker, rolling with her as another creature leapt for them.

Her fingers brushed the pillar, grasping for him at the same time. The same shifting of atoms raining through the dark night. Something drained away from him at the same time and he landed with a thump into brown leaves. Perrette landed on top of him, her head connecting with his chest and driving the air out of his lungs.

They lay with tangled limbs, each panting their nightmare experience out. Tomas stared at the black streaks of branches and twigs across the clear blue sky and found his hands were automatically cradling the woman on top of him, his fingers twitching as if they were ready to go exploring without permission. They were too close, she was warm and soft and all in the right places. The dark mass of hair was inviting him to bury his face in it, its musk invading his nostrils. He rolled them over and released her reluctantly.

Perrette blinked and tugged the hair out of her face. "Fuck." She stared at him and flushed slightly. "Someone's taken a good fifteen years off you." She reached up as if she might brush his hair back and stopped herself.

Tomas grunted and stood to get away from her disturbing presence. He grabbed for his trousers and more as he stood up, the weight of the belt nearly exposing him to the cool air. He'd forgotten he lost weight with a younger body.

Perrette gave an unexpectedly dirty chuckle, "Don't mind me."

He responded in kind, pausing as he did his belt up, "Fancy a look do you?"

"Oh you know, seen one dick, seen them all…" Her response was deliberately casual as she turned her back to look at the view. Tomas huffed in amusement and pulled his belt tighter. The clothes now looked odd on him, too old for his younger, fitter frame. He wondered why she'd taken the years off him so quickly, she had changed his age before but it was still unusual unless there was a reason. His current passport would be too old for him, he'd have to go back to his previous one and began swearing when he remembered, it was in his bunker with the rest of his baggage. He glanced around, it looked like early afternoon, plenty of time for those men to have taken every scrap of personal information he'd left there.

A call interrupted his vile mood and he saw that Perrette had wandered to the top of the hill. Tomas hurried over to see and swore at what she was pointing at. The stream still ran through the valley but his bunker had disappeared. Hazard tape cut off the large bite taken out of the earth, trees were down, their roots waving at the sky, the large stones entangled adding to the general devastation.

"Fuck…" he breathed.

"What happened?"

"That explosion as we came through, it must have been the munitions pile in the other bunker, the one connected to mine. It had partially collapsed from the second world war, that spray of bullets must have caught something."

There was a tent standing in amongst the trees looking like an afterthought and the police were shepherding the local youth away from gawping. He'd always thought she would do something if that pile had exploded, he'd not expected to be dragged into another world though.

"What about that man, would he have survived?" Tomas grabbed her arm, "He was one of us, wasn't he."

Perrette went white, "Please, you have your secrets, I have mine. I can't tell you certain things okay?" There was something wrong, the set of her mouth and the way her eyes had creased. He nodded slowly. She continued, her voice shaking, "I doubt he got out or the other one. They weren't that important and we had two gods pulling us. I think that's why we ended up at such an obscure way marker, if it had just been Dar, he'd have brought me to one I recognised." Tomas stared at her and she set her lips, "Please believe me…"

He nodded sharply, "Fine, you can't talk." Tomas started walking, leaving her staring and ignored her scrambling after him.

"What are you going to do?"

"None of your business, you got me back so our bargain is finished."

Walking with this younger body was a pleasure and his stride lengthened. He nodded absently to the police officer walking down the lane in the knowledge that he wouldn't be recognised as the older man he had been and two steps later swore to himself. He had no identification, no passport or driving licence. His wallet had been on the table with the laptop and his phone. He didn't even have the paperwork for his other identity, even if he was five years too young for it.

Tomas stopped, his shoulders slumped. He was going to have to work his way through the transient communities, scraping money together until he could afford to pay for an illegal boat over the channel and get to his other persona. He patted his jeans pockets looking for anything he could use. The pocket that had had the USB in had ripped, the other crackled. He pulled out the photo the inspector had given him and turned it to see the phone number scrawled in black ink.

"What's that?" Perrette was peering over his shoulder.

Tomas stuffed it back, "Nothing. Have you got any money or a phone I could use?"

"No."

"Right." He turned and marched determinedly towards the houses.

Even his legs were aching when they reached the village square, they were both looking creased and worse for the wear. Perrette had stopped trying to engage him in conversation and had doggedly shadowed him all the way.

Tomas was relieved to see the little café open. "Stay quiet," he ordered. Perrette pulled a face at his tone and followed him in. The young waitress was flicking a cloth over one of the tables, he was pleased to see business was quiet.

"Hello, do you remember serving me yesterday with my friend?" The waitress blinked at his younger self. He smiled, "I was practising for a part and was made up to look like an older man – did it work? We left you a large tip."

Her jaw dropped, "That was you?"

Tomas feigned embarrassment and shrugged, "You commented on my picture." He showed her the photo and she laughed, searching his face and he was relieved to see the beginnings of recognition. "My problem is that I've mislaid my phone, could I use yours? I need to make a single call to my friend."

"Well… customers aren't really allowed…" She glanced towards the door.

"It'll just be a quick one." He hoped it would be.

She gave in, looking at the door all the time. Her boss must be out Tomas decided. He rang the number on the back, shifting from foot to foot as it rang.

Stef answered, sounding tired, "Yes?"

"It's Tomas. You were right." There was a stunned silence on the other end. He ignored Perrette's sharpening look. "I've got no phone or I.D. Can you help?"

"There was an explosion."

"Yes." He repeated, "Can you help?"

Stef sounded rattled, "Where are you?"

"In the same café we spoke in yesterday. I've no money either."

"I'll get a cab to pick you up. I've a flat in London."

"That's going to cost you a fair bit." It was miles, the cab's meter would be working overtime.

"You'd better make it worth it, I want to know what happened out there. I told you…"

"Yes, I know. I'll be waiting." He clicked the off button and put the phone down on the counter. "Thank you," he smiled at the waitress and winked as an older woman came bustling into the café. The waitress gave him a hesitant smile back and busied herself at the table.

The older woman asked, "Can I help you sir?"

"No thank you, we were just leaving." Tomas widened the smile to include her and herded Perrette out of the door. They paused just outside to see a couple of coaches disgorging tourists into the tiny square.

"What the fuck was all that about?" Perrette demanded.

"I've no I.D., no money and no phone. I need a way to get money at least. I have people looking for me, helped by yourself." He mustered a glare at her, their truce was off as far as he was concerned. “Why are you asking, do you want to come with me?”

Perrette turned away, tightening her lips. The tension was back in her body, he could tell she was withholding something. She said, “They’ll find you.”

“There’s one place where they won’t look.”

“Where?”

Tomas’ face was grim, he wasn’t going to tell her who he was going to. He didn’t even know where Stef was taking him. “The authorities.”

She quietly exploded, glancing at the tourists moving in knots and pointing at the honey coloured houses. “What the fuck are you talking about? They are the authorities. They have power everywhere, haven’t you realised that?”

“There’s a man I met recently, he’s a detective and his curiosity bump is bigger than his rational brain can cope with.”

“How the fuck do you not know he’s working for them? They’ve got contacts and people on a scale you can’t comprehend.”

“I don’t and I’m pleased you do but it’ll confuse the hell out of them if he is working for them.” He’d work something out, London was a far better place to be than this isolated rural spot where you were either a local or a stranger. “Are you coming?”

“No.” She ducked her head, not looking at him.

“What’s stopping me from making you stay?” He snapped hold of her wrist. She knew what he could do, he didn’t need to threaten further.

Perrette went white and said softly, “Because of the look in your eyes when you kissed me under the arch at Ticha.”

Tomas’ jaw dropped and he barely noticed his fingers slackening. That bridge… so many years ago, the warmth of the body in his arms, hers twining around his neck. He'd left shortly afterwards unable to cope with the thought of seeing her aging… What the fuck? That had been two hundred and fifty years ago at least. He started to say something and found Perrette had disappeared, ducking into the crowd of tourists.

Chapter 9

A cab drew up while he was still gaping.

"Mr Horvat?"

Tomas shook himself, "Yes?"

"I'm supposed to take you to London." Distracted, Tomas agreed and ignored the cab driver's attempts at conversation until he gave it up as a bad job.

Those eyes, the first time he'd seen them was so long ago, centuries before he'd kissed her under that bridge. Could this actually be the same woman he'd been coming across every time? He flicked through those meetings, how many times his eyes had picked her out and recognised her amongst the millions of others.

He cast his mind back and thought carefully through each encounter. At every point she'd had an older man with her, he'd not thought it strange at the time, women historically didn't tend to live without some male company to vouch for them. He'd typically only spend a few days around before he'd disappear, not wanting to cause a scandal but had that actually stopped him from being caught?

The longest he'd spent had been that time culminating under the bridge. Had those coy glances, the whispered promises been true? Tomas clenched his fists, remembering the dark hair covered modestly with a coif and the eyes sparking a shy mischief under the cover of a respectable merchant's wife. She'd played him like a lute, drawing him towards her, pretending to worry about her reputation. He'd ignored his god's warnings at that point, heated by the kisses they'd exchanged and he'd nearly got caught by the town's bailiffs on a trumped up charge.

Had that really been the intention? What had they intended to do to him? When he'd snuck back several years later and in the guise of middle age she'd not been there anymore, not that he'd wanted more than a glance to check that she was safe. Had she really been hunting him for this long? Too many questions bubbled over the hours he'd spent in wistful thinking, knowing that he would have to watch her grow old turned into an anger that there'd been no need, that she'd been like him and known it.

Tomas chewed a thumbnail, and who were these people after him? He muttered a swear word to himself, ignoring the cab driver's glance in the rear view mirror. He should have kept her with him and made her answer some questions. Was she right about the authorities chasing him? He had a feeling that Stef was honest. Tomas ransacked his brain to make sure he wasn't clouding his judgment and decided that it was right, that man was too straight. Tomas reached into his pocket to look at the photo again and couldn't find it. He patted down his pockets – nothing.

He was sure he'd kept hold of it at the café, had he put it into his pocket correctly? He shook his head, he'd have to leave it. The sun was beginning to set and a spatter of rain made the wipers begin. The sound lulled him and he half closed his eyes, staring at the darkening sky. The image of a woman built behind him, he knew better than to turn – she wouldn't be there.

"My Tomas." The words were silent. She brushed her fingers through his dark hair and smiled her benediction. He bowed his head, feeling the weight of her arms across his shoulders and was unable to stop the tears rising. He was still her favoured.

"I will come and find you one day my lady." Tomas spoke into the silence of his soul and she closed her eyes, becoming the flash of a car's headlights in the rain. He decided to put his faith into his gut feeling, she wouldn't abandon him.

He dozed for the rest of the journey, waking fully when they came off the motorway and into the city's brighter lights. They wound their way through the streets ending up on a council estate. Tomas stared at the low-rise buildings of only five or six floors, this was luxury in comparison to the crowded tenancy he'd lived in.

"I was told to tell you it's number one hundred and thirty five. It's on the ground floor in the third building along. He's paid me already." The cab driver was short and no doubt pleased to be rid of his taciturn passenger. Tomas grunted his thanks and walked off.

The noise of the city rose about him, it was late evening and the lives of many people buzzed close by. The rain had cleared as they'd travelled, clearing to a starlit evening. He smiled, the peace of the countryside was nice enough but he preferred to lose himself amongst others. A few other people were around, mostly the local youth lurking in groups and no doubt inadvertently terrorising the older generations. Nothing jarred as being out of the ordinary. The flat was easy enough to find, the numbers painted on the outside door. He took a deep breath and rang the bell. Stef's voice let him in and directed him across the corridor to an unremarkable door.

Stef opened it when he knocked and stared. "Well, if I hadn't guessed before then this really is showing me what you can do."

Tomas shrugged, "Can I come in?" The other man stood aside, still staring. Tomas took in the room, everything was neat and in its place, there was very little to show any character. "I was right, you are a sad bastard."

Stef chuckled, "This isn't home, it's a place I have for just in case. Besides, you're the sad bastard wearing an old man's clothes." Tomas grinned and looked at Stef carefully, there was no smart suit this time, the jeans and jumper were crumpled and the boots worn. Stef relaxed against the door frame, unworried by his scrutiny. The atmosphere had relaxed into two men of a similar age winding each other up.

"Have you got anything I could steal?"

"Hang on, I'll have a look." Stef went into another room and Tomas heard the sound of drawers opening. He came out, "On the bed."

The room was in a similar state, no pictures on the walls or books on the single shelf and the bed was neatly made up, barely a crease in the duvet. The trousers he found still needed a belt but they were far more manageable, Tomas slung his own shirt back over the logo'ed t-shirt he borrowed and came out to smell coffee brewing.

"You take it black don't you?" Tomas nodded. "So, why did you ring me? I didn't expect to hear from you after that explosion." Tomas automatically reached for the packet of cigarettes in his shirt pocket and hesitated. "I don't mind, go ahead." A saucer was found and pushed towards him.

Tomas sat back and let the smoke fill his lungs, pleased that they'd survived the transition. "You were right about the bodies piling up sooner or later. I came to this country looking for a bit of peace. It didn't happen."

"How did you manage to get out of the bunker? There were several bodies burnt beyond recognition, I assumed one was you." Stef slurped his coffee.

"Sad for me?"

Stef retorted, "Right pissed off more likely. I thought I'd got you."

"You had." Tomas smiled and let out a long breath, watching the smoke coil. "Every one of those photos is of me. I try to stay off the radar but it's beginning to prove difficult."

"I can imagine, how do you do this?" He gestured at Tomas.

Tomas hesitated and thought why not? He'd not told anyone before and it felt right with this man despite Perrette's concerns. She'd proven to be the untrustworthy one. "Do you believe in fairy tales Stef?" He used the other man's given name deliberately.

"I believe they were used as a way of warning people while amusing them around the fireside – why?"

"Let me tell you a fairy tale." Tomas stretched slightly, sitting up straight to command his audience of one. "In times long ago when life was hard and gods were plentiful there lived a youth with his many younger sisters and parents. His mother was kind, his father was blessed with a small talent for making bowls and they were poor but happy." He caught Stef's look of amusement at the way he'd started and ignored it, he could only tell this story by divorcing himself from his own life.

"The youth began to learn his father's trade from an early age, in those times children were considered a useful pair of hands and part of the working society. Shortly after he became what would be now known as a teenager, his father fell ill. His stomach swelled and he was unable to eat or make the bowls that had kept the family alive. The youth took over to keep the orders coming in, he tried hard but couldn't make them as well as his father and the customers stopped.

"As I said, the family were poor but somehow they scraped money together to pay for a doctor. He gave them medicine which cost more money and promised it would work. The father became worse and the doctor refused to answer his door when they tried to complain, his servants turning them away and threatening to set the dogs on them if they came back. The mother went to the priests, they wailed over the father with them and told her to accept the judgment of the gods. The mother withdrew, becoming thin herself in sorrow.

"The youth refused to believe that the gods could take his father away from him. He went from temple to shrine, pleading for some intervention and was turned away from all of them. The father fought the illness, becoming a yellowing skeleton with a round stomach and the little sisters were shadows of their former selves."

Part of Tomas was aware of Stef leaning forwards, his mouth open and holding back the questions. He himself was too involved, remembering the smell of the tiny hovel he had lived in, the sickness and the sorrow. He stubbed out the ashes of his cigarette, the scent reminiscent of burnt offerings.

"There was only charity to support those unable to help themselves in those days and the youth would make his rounds every day despite his misplaced pride. He hated the begging and abject mutterings he would have to give to his betters for money or bread. A whisper of a rumour caught him in his search one day. There was a shrine from an old god several miles away, it hadn't been worshipped for years. The youth decided that he would visit it. No other gods had helped him, maybe this one would. He settled his family, reassuring his little sisters that he would be back and left.

"The shrine was further than he'd thought, over hills and streams, many miles from where they lived. He eventually found it in a wood, a tall stone standing next to a pool so circular it was perfection. He'd walked all day and half the night to get there and the moon was high and as round as the pool. He fell flat on his face and beseeched the god to help him."

Tomas moistened his lips with the coffee, his voice rough as he said, "The god answered his prayers and came to him." He closed his eyes briefly, he daren't talk about the vision he'd had. The beautiful dark eyed woman reaching out to run her hand through his tangled hair. He'd never so much as felt a sniff of holiness in any of the other temples or shrines. This place had reeked of something else, was it a sanctity? Whatever it was, it had made his hair stand on end.

He cleared his throat, "The god listened to the youth's problems and offered a choice. She would either heal his father so he could live a healthy life to die in old age or she would take the father under her wing and allow him to die peacefully and painlessly.

"The youth wanted his father, he knew he couldn't support his beloved family. He wanted his mother to sing again, his sisters to be happy. It felt so little to ask. He offered to worship the god if she would do this and the god accepted his offer." The warmth in her eyes as she'd listened, the attention she'd given him – he should have known… Tomas' hand was shaking as he picked up the mug again.

The silence went on too long and Stef asked hesitantly, "What happened? Did the father die?"

Tomas took a deep breath, "The youth walked back the many miles to his family and found that his father had opened his eyes and drunk some of the thin soup the youth had left for his family. As the days progressed, he became stronger and his stomach smaller although he never lost it. The youth's mother began to smile again and it was declared a tiny miracle in the poor community.

"The youth was overjoyed. He made a tiny shrine in the corner of the room where they slept, a bowl of water and a candle that he would take outside in the dead of night to pray over, casting his meagre offerings to the winds." Tomas tossed the last of the coffee down, the bitter dregs matching his mood.

Stef's mouth dropped, "Is that it? What…" He began to say more when his phone beeped. "What do they fucking want now?" He pulled it out and stared, "Runp? What the fuck does that mean?"

"What?" Tomas reached over to grab the other man's wrist and swivelled the phone round so he could see the screen. The message was clear to him – Run P. He swung around to peer between the curtains at the front window and saw blue lights in the distance - cars were gathering across the front of the green. "Shit." He glared at Stef, "Did you do this?"

Stef came to look through the gap and narrowed his eyes, "Nothing to do with me, we need to leave." He grabbed for Tomas' arm. "There's a fire exit in the back of the building. We'll go that way."

"Why should I trust you?"

The other man looked at him as though he was stupid, "You're one in a million. No, more than that. I want to know about you."

"And the bodies?"

"I've been around murderers, you get a feel for people, it's part of my job. You're not one of them."

Tomas nodded slowly. "The way out?" Stef threw him a coat and grabbed another for himself. The lights could be seen clearly through the window next to the front door, the fire exit was at the other end of the corridor. Tomas hesitated, his hand hovering over the bar.

"It's not connected to anything, we had several incidents where people were setting it off, the council got fed up of the complaints." Stef grinned and pushed it open.

They slid through the exit, Tomas could see the lights across the grass to both sides of the building bobbing as the men walked.

"They'll be trying to cover all exits, luckily it's too open to do that. Here." Stef reached into his pocket and brought out a phone and his wallet. He pulled out a wad of bank notes and tried to hand Tomas the phone as well.

"Thanks, I'll take the money for the moment and pay you back. The phone you can keep." They'd be able to track the phone, thankfully paper money was still accepted in most places. He'd be able to get another phone and live off grid while he decided how to get off this island.

They stopped in the shadow of another building and watched the line of policemen advancing. The youths had disappeared, baiting policemen not being in their remit. Tomas wondered if this was what Perrette had meant, who could possibly want him who was this high up? Tomas flinched as he heard his name announced over the loud speakers, the residents being asked to stay inside.

"There are still gaps but you'll need balls of steel to get through them." Stef swore as they heard another sound over the hum of traffic. "They've brought the fucking helicopter, it's got infra-red on it - see that gap? Run now."

Stef broke away, running in the opposite direction to the way he'd been pointing and Tomas saw a dog loosed in the sweep of light from the helicopter and swore. Stef was about the same size as him, he was trying to draw them off.

Acting on a benevolence he rarely had, Tomas raced after the other man, reaching out to his god. He didn't know how to do this, didn't know if it was going to work. The loudspeaker was hailing him, telling him to stand still with his hands up over the noise of the blades in the air. His own breathing was coming hard in his ears as Stef turned to look while he ran, complete disbelief on his face when he saw Tomas behind him.

The dog was running towards them, its teeth gleaming and ears back. The searchlight found them and lit up the grass making him wince. Surrounded by a radiance not of his own making, Tomas grasped for Stef's arm and pulled him close. Now, he thought and reached out for his god.

Chapter 10

This time Tomas was expecting the disassembly, he kept hold of Stef throughout and landed in a pile with him. He was upright immediately looking around and trying to gauge any apparent threats. The mist swirled as it had done before and the inhuman clicks and screeches in the distance were just as unnerving. He was relived to find the ground solid under his feet and the way marker taller than he was. He reached out in curiosity, wondering if it was cool to touch and stopped himself – he didn't want to go back through just yet.

Stef pulled himself on his hands and knees and promptly threw up. "Fuck," he said, spitting noisily.

"Yeah, it takes a bit of getting used to."

The other man sat back on his heels and looked around as he spat onto the grass. "Okay, explain."

"Apparently this is the Hall. I dragged us here to get away from pursuit although I've only been here once before and it's dangerous as well in its own sweet way."

"What's here apart from trees and mist?" Stef shuddered at one of the stranger sounds, "And other things I don't want to know about?"

"The gods." Tomas turned his back to the post and spotted the track leading towards the larger trees. "Stay close, you don't want to fall through some of the gaps." At Stef's confused look he explained, "Some of what you can see appears to be an illusion, the ground goes soggy. Step carefully." Stef widened his eyes and watched his feet, placing them where Tomas did.

The gap between the trees materialized and Tomas felt his breathing relax, this was one place he didn't want to get lost. Still wary of holes, he walked that bit faster with Stef beside him. He could see Stef was as fascinated as he'd been by the vagueness of the scenery and how the detail slid from the eye even when you came close. The track began to open up, the Corridor was ahead and gleaming pale in the ever present half-light. Tomas peered both ways, worried. He didn't know this place half as well as he needed to.

A whisper of a warning and Tomas pulled Stef back and down, putting his finger to his lips. They sprawled in the damp grass waiting, ears and eyes straining for any movement. Tomas was just about to admit that the warning must have been a false alarm when there was a rush of syncopated footsteps. Both he and Stef ducked down further, peering out between two tussocks.

Shadowy figures flickered, strobing up the path, never in the same position twice and never seen fully. Hands gestured and heads nodded, the feet never appearing to touch the ground. It was a crowd, appearing larger than life against the black trees, snatches of conversation half heard. As the party passed, the ground rumbled under them, shifting in a sea wave. Tomas had the sense of the whole landscape shifting to suit the party's journey and he remembered Perrette saying how the locations of the gods changed.

Fingers grasped his arm tightly and Tomas glanced at Stef, his face looked green and he was struggling not to throw up again. The figures were still going past - they couldn't call attention to themselves. Stef had his eyes shut tight and concentrating. Tomas clung onto his own sanity at the chaos happening in front of them. He swore that one of them turned to look in their direction and he smashed both their faces into the grass.

The last of the figures disappeared and the normal sounds of the woods resumed. Tomas let the tension out of his shoulders and heard Stef still flat on his face and vomiting into the grass.

"You okay?"

"I'm not keen on this place." Stef rolled over, wiping his mouth. "What was that?"

"Who not what and no, I don't know."

They came to the end of the track, Tomas stopping Stef from stepping onto it. Perrette had said that people would know if they travelled on it but also that it could be dangerous not to. His pulling them both into this world may have announced that they were there and people might be looking for them. He closed his eyes and reached out. The clear line leading him to her, he could feel her reaching out as well this time.

"Come on, this way." He stepped onto the Corridor and began walking, Stef beside him. Stef kept rubbing his eyes as they walked. "What's up?"

"This bloody place, everything moves in ways it shouldn't. Doesn't anything stay still?"

Tomas blinked, he'd already got used to it. The way trees and rocks slid into middle distance depending on whether you were looking or not, the wind moving the mist but not the branches. There was a large white stone, cracked down the middle close to them, it sidled closer as he took a step. He watched it for a moment bemused. "Do you want to walk with your eyes shut for a bit? I'll…" He was speaking to thin air, Stef was walking as though in a dream towards the track next to the stone. "Hang on, you can't walk down there." Stef ignored him, a smile on his face. Tomas grabbed his arm to be shaken off.

"He wants me…"

"Like hell he does." Tomas found himself lashing the line of light connecting him to his own god around him tightly and using it as an anchor, pulled Stef away. The other man fought him, insisting that he was wanted.

Tomas ignored him and dragged him several steps down the path, away from the track.

Abruptly, Stef stopped fighting and his legs gave way. "He wanted me…" His face held a desolation as he sprawled on the cobbles.

Tomas knelt in front of him and shook his shoulder, "Look, you don't want to go down there. That stone's cracked, I reckon he's dead. You don't want to end up like me or worse."

Stef's face slowly cleared, "He was so sad."

"I know, I've had the same and I've got a god. They can't help it."

The other man scrubbed his face and held out a hand to be pulled up. Tomas grunted, Stef wasn't a lightweight and he reckoned he'd have several bruises from him swinging his fists. Stef took a step forwards, his whole body angling towards the stone and shuddered. "Distract me while we walk, tell me the rest of your story."

Tomas sighed, he'd hoped not to do this. Still, if it kept Stef alive then it would be worth it. "Okay, but did you know you've a hole in your arse?"

"What?" Stef clapped a hand over his backside and found a huge rip from where his mobile phone had been. "Shit, I've dropped it."

Tomas found himself sniggering, "Modern technology doesn't come here. Didn't you notice the breeze?"

"Arse yourself." Stef hitched his trousers up, "At least there's no one else here to see. So, start talking."

Tomas put a hand on Stef's shoulder to keep them together and found himself pulling on the line between himself and his god while they walked. The landscape moved faster as he pulled and he wondered if this was what the figures they'd seen earlier had been doing.

He mentally brought himself back to the point where he'd left off, restarting the nightmare. "A year went by with the youth learning more of his father's trade which became popular due to his miraculous recovery, his sisters grew fatter and happier and his mother sang as she worked in the house. The youth noticed nothing wrong until his voice changed."

Tomas could feel Stef's eyes on him and daren't look, caught in the horror of his own recollection. "His voice began to wobble, sliding from a young man's tenor to a child's treble. When he finally noticed, other changes became more apparent, his clothes had become loose, he no longer filled the shirts his father had given him and he had lost hair on the parts of his body that had declared him on the way to manhood.

"He carried on, not wanting to accept the changes until the time came when he had no choice. People were looking at him sidelong, walking past him on the other side of the street and those that had frequented his father's shop now avoided it. He railed at the tiny shrine he had made but the god refused to answer so he determined to visit the standing stone in the glade and confront her.

"He walked the many miles back. It felt further to his child's body, the dangers more apparent minus the teenage bravissimo of before. He waited, shivering at the pool for the moon to rise and realised in the dark that it was a new moon that night. She came to him as he slept in exhaustion, running her hand through his hair and smiling possessively. The boy woke and demanded to know what she had done to him, his fists clenched and voice shrill in the night."

He remembered the way her eyes had darkened, the unseen light glinting off the porcelain skin and the frown appearing between her perfect eyebrows. "'Is your father better?' The boy nodded and she cut off his protests. 'I fulfilled my promise which means you are mine, complete your side of the bargain - you promised to worship me.' The hidden thunder behind the words threatened.

"The boy objected, hadn't he made a shrine? Given her offerings? He cast around desperately, did she want him to stay here with her? Keep her company or go out into the world and exhort people to pray to her? His father was well, his family could do without him although he would miss them.

"She laughed at his simple ideas. 'Do you even know which god I am or how one worships me?' At the look on his face she continued, 'I am Al-Kiron, the god of death and you are my disciple. I demand that my worshippers give me lives to satisfy my hunger.'

"The cold realisation came to the boy all at once and he shivered, tears running down his face. She leant forwards, a terrible compassion radiating from her. 'I will give you another choice, let it not be said that I forced you into this.'

"The boy's hopes crumbled at her next words. 'You may choose to worship me in the way I wish for the rest of your life or we will conclude our bargain now. A life for a life. I will gather you into my arms and your father will live his long and happy life, your sisters will marry well and your parents will die sleeping together in their bed, fulfilled.' She held her hand out, the unseen light glinting off the dark depths of her eyes.

"It was no choice to the boy. As a child he held a horror of death he couldn't shake off. Gathering his courage he asked, 'You want me to kill people for you? How? With this body I am too small to fight.'

"'I will give you the means. Weapons, poison or mishaps are not required, you will touch them and they will fall under my spell, painlessly.' She considered him stood there, his small shoulders slumped in defeat. 'And do not think that you can deny me. If you refuse to worship me in the way I require, while others grow older, you will grow younger until you are a puling baby and I will take you anyway.'

"The boy bowed his head in agreement as the dark moon passed over the pool and she disappeared, satisfied in his capitulation. He fell asleep next to it and woke in the morning in an empty glade. He walked to the next village late the next morning, his heart frozen in grief. He watched the villagers in their daily life from the hill above, waiting for the sun to go down. When the first of the men came out of the tavern that night, the boy was there. The man fell without a cry at his feet and the god smiled over his shoulder in the lanternlight.

"The village was talked about for years afterwards, about the night death walked its streets. No one was spared, babies in cribs, people in the houses, all were found dead. Only the animals were left alive, cows lowed in their byres, dogs barking on their chains and rats slinking through the thatch. No one could understand what had happened, it was left to disappear into the countryside."

There was a long pause before Tomas said, "And the boy walked away, no longer a boy but a man of middle years, cursed to walk the earth forever more."

Tomas bowed his head, remembering waking that day in an unfamiliar body, the silent village around him and the horror of his god's delight in the offerings he'd given her. He felt the tug of the line between them, today he would meet her at last on her own territory. What could he say to her that he hadn't already said so many times in the silence of his heart?

"I'm so sorry."

He remembered the man walking beside him. Stef's face was full of compassion. Tomas turned his head away and grunted, "We're nearly there."

A track like any other, he stopped at the moss streaked rock, anticipation clenching his stomach at the chance finally to see her. A movement beside him broke his concentration, Stef had that look again. He shook the other man's shoulder, "She's a god of death, remember that."

Stef blinked, "Not 'The God of Death'?"

Tomas said slowly. "I don't think so, I don't know how it works, I just know she's a god, that's all." So little he knew about her considering he'd been shackled to her for so many centuries. She'd never offered any more information and he'd never asked, too wrapped up in his own misery. He'd railed against her, begged at times, pleaded, equally terrified that she would take away what she'd given and yet hating what he did to stay alive. The hubbub came up through the years, threatening to drown him. Voices, gestures, he whirled in a black pit, sinking ever deeper. He panicked, the human mind wasn't made to comprehend such a long existence. A firm hand clapped on to his own, still resting on the other man's shoulder.

He blinked, brought back from the well of memories by a simple human touch. "So many years…" The words slipped out before he could stop them.

"And somehow you've kept going." Stef's words reminded him of his shameful secret.

"Let's get this over with." Tomas squared his shoulders and walked down the track, the line between them becoming thicker with every step.

The track opened out into a glade, the trees lining it. The peculiar half-light of the Hall lit up the perfectly circular pool in the middle and the standing stone to the side. Tomas felt his breath catch - there was a statue of a woman facing them, her head bowed and her hands spread in benediction.

The statue was of alabaster, he recognised the face of the god who had granted his wish so many years ago, the hands held out as if ready to take a supplicant to her bosom. He could almost feel the crumbled remains of those that had fallen before her in the march of the years. There was a soft glow around her, the line connecting them was the same and he knew without being told that it showed that she still had a worshipper – himself. Without thinking, he fell to his knees, taking Stef with him.

"My lady."

He didn't know how long he stayed there, his face pressed into the grass as the feeling in the glade began to change. Tomas raised his head at the brush of fingers across his hair and sat back on his heels, tears streaking his face. Stef appeared frozen, facedown, in position.

This was the glade he had sworn himself in, somehow she'd brought it to him when he'd needed her. The atmosphere was heavy, reeking like an incense filled church. A half-moon appeared in the pool and he had to stop himself checking the sky – it wouldn't be there – he knew that now.

"Tomas." The statue was still there but she was elsewhere. His eyes darted around and found her slender shape in the shadow of the standing stone. Al-Kiron peeled herself away and walked towards him. She loomed above him, miles tall and yet was slender and fragile. He squashed his urge to protect her. "Is your ego still so sore my beloved?"

"You know how I feel." The years of killing simply to stay alive, the pain, the living in places where atrocities were common. His soul felt old and dirty.

"Humans are bound to so many ideals, in love and in concept. Is what we have so different?" Tomas turned his face away, struggling between being in the presence of his god and the things he had to do to stay alive. "You have the same choice as you ever did. I will take you if you cannot cope."

He couldn't be anything less than honest in front of her. "I tried..." Tears spilled down his face – he'd tried. Refusing to take someone's life until he'd become a child again, his body shrinking and his fears growing. He persevered, the years leaving him faster until one night he'd snapped without realising it, the childish part of his brain taking over. He'd woken in the body of a young man, dead people all around him. After that he'd gone on into a rampaging despair, killing everyone until he was a shank limbed shuffling old man and even then...

He'd stopped at the final death. He couldn't do it, couldn't sink into the black oblivion, his soul screaming inside to live. Tomas had collapsed into a heap and she'd left him to contemplate what he'd done, fat and replete with the worship he'd given her. "I met another favoured, she brought me here. She said her god is Dar."

"Dar is a god of mischief."

"I don't know whether to trust her or not. She's close to people who appear to be hunting me." Tomas glanced at Stef, unsure whether to say more. Stef appeared frozen, his face staring at the grass by his knees.

Al-Kiron dismissed the still figure, "You must be wary of her, her way of worship is to twist and slide from the truth."

"I guessed that," he said dryly. She wasn't telling him much more than he already knew.

"Still, she protects her own as you do. You must protect me Tomas. Without you I am nothing."

Him protect her? That was new, he was the one at her mercy. All this time and he had simply survived through it, lurching from one situation to another. She could change the rules that allowed him to keep his body and by consequence his mind stable and she frequently did. It was a pain in these days of concrete identification. The constant monitoring of himself, checking to make sure he hadn't changed in a way that would be noticeable. A cold thought crossed his mind, what would happen if she chose to abandon him? All she needed to do was find a worshipper more devoted, more tractable and that would be the end of him. He squashed down both jealousy and fear.

As though reading his mind she turned to Stef's still figure and smiled. "Who is this?"

Answers jumbled through Tomas' head, all too long and none of them quite right. "He's a friend." Pleased with his answer, her smile widened and she gestured at Stef. He blinked and shook his head as though waking from a dream. Glancing up, he saw her and his mouth fell open. He stumbled to his feet and nodded awkwardly.

Tomas recognised the look, and felt the insidious creeping of the glade moving towards the other man. "No… you can't…"

Al-Kiron's voice sharpened, he recognised it from the times she'd chastised him as a child. "What you want is immaterial. You managed well to get him here however he is unlikely to get back without going mad or being taken by another. Look into the pool to see what he will become if this happens."

Tomas stood and walked over to the pool. He was reminded of the dream he'd had in the hospital, gazing into the dark depths and had to hold himself tightly to stop himself from swaying. The half moon diffused as he gazed downward, spreading its light to form a scene.

He saw broken stones in a pile, the white gleam suggesting the markers on the Corridor and a figure appeared, his hands held over his face, plainly screaming though there was no sound. The skin withered over the hands, twisting the flesh, the clothes hanging off the once stocky frame until finally the figure dropped his hands to slump, his head bowed. Tomas barely recognised his friend, the eyes vacant, skin and flesh hanging off him. He was joined by others in the same state, all moving in the same direction. They were funnelling into a track of grass off the path and a further horror rose without knowing why. He pulled himself away and began retching dryly. Stef was still staring at Al-Kiron when Tomas finally had his stomach under control.

Tomas asked, “If he becomes yours, then he’ll be safe from this?”

She flicked her eyes at him, “He will be safer.” That was no answer and they both knew it. Al-Kiron drew herself up and stretched out a hand, “He has already made his choice and you have no part in it. Stefan Ludwick, I make a claim on you. You will become one of my favoured. Kneel before me and receive my blessing.”

Stef stepped towards her and fell to his knees beside Tomas. He saw tears stream down the other man’s face and the sudden gleam of light encircling them both.

Chapter 11

The landscape was far more prosaic here, tall brick built terraces with tiny gardens facing the neon lit streets. Cars lined the road and it was one of those odd times of the evening when all was quiet. Tomas had paid off the taxi driver a few streets away, the instincts of years making him prefer to walk the last short distance unobserved.

"We were lucky I gave you that money before we left." Stef yawned as they walked. Tomas grunted, keeping an eye on the dark cars parked on both sides. "I didn't fancy getting the tube halfway across London with my arse hanging out. It's too cold."

Tomas hadn't had the chance to interrogate Al-Kiron like he'd wanted to, stunned as he'd been by her taking Stef as one of her own. He shoved down the squirming feeling that he wasn't on his own any more, he didn't want to analyse it. Glancing up at the numbers picked out in brass on every door, he asked, "What number are you?"

"Forty five. God I feel good." Stef almost giggled at his choice of words and Tomas rolled his eyes, struggling to contain his disapproval despite knowing Stef couldn't do much about it. Al-Kiron had sent pyrotechnics across Stef's brain and he'd been sky high since they'd left. That sort of state was only fun if you'd shared the drinking session and were in a similar mess.

"Key." Tomas held out his hand and had it slapped in. He hesitated and lowered his voice, "Are you sure it's forty five?"

"Yes, I've lived there for several years. Lovely neighbours this side, he's an engineer and she's got the biggest set of…"

Tomas shushed him. "Is there a way in through the back?"

Stef sobered slightly, bringing his hands down from where they were gesturing. "Yes, there's an access road at the end of the street. What's up?" Tomas hooked a hand through Stef's arm to stop him pausing and walked him past number forty five.

"Was it daylight when you left?"

"Yes."

"Then you wouldn't have left the upstairs light on, would you?" Stef's mouth dropped and Tomas could see him struggling to think. So much for the great detective.

The unlit access road was just large enough for them both to walk down together. The yards were small on each side, the houses crowding close. Lights from the houses made the shadows deeper and Tomas was too aware that it would be a perfect place for an ambush. Bins had been put out for the next day and lined the fences haphazardly, avoiding them wasn't easy. A scrabbling made them both jump and Stef snorted at the cat appearing and the thud of it landing on a bin.

Tomas counted the gates off, noting the ones with numbers, "This one yours? Do you keep it locked?" He could clearly see the kitchen light on, shining into the small back courtyard.

"Bolted," Stef nodded. Tomas muttered a swear word and dragged a bin across. He made short work of clearing the gate and threw the bolts to let Stef in. They crouched down and watched the window. A slim figure walked past in the hall.

"There's someone still there."

Stef was struggling to concentrate through his brain throwing fireworks, "I do have a work friend who has a key, it could be Chris. He waits for me sometimes although he normally gives a ring." He patted his ripped pocket, "Saying that, I wouldn't know if he had this time."

"We'll soon find out," Tomas said grimly - that figure hadn't looked like a man. He shot across the yard, avoiding the metal table and chairs and slid the key into the lock, twisting it silently. He was almost looking forward to finding out who the intruder was and dealing with him. He didn't want to think about the yawning chasm of jealousy Stef's conversion had left.

The kitchen was tiny and sparsely furnished, a plant was hanging on hopefully for water on the kitchen window. The thought flicked through his mind that he'd been right, Stef was a sad bastard. Not giving any time for the breeze of the back door opening to warn anyone, Tomas slid around the hall door, all senses on high alert. He stepped lightly on the tiled floor, he didn't want to give anyone the chance to get to Stef. Tomas knew he'd likely had some form of combat training, but in his state… A whisper of a movement and Tomas jerked upright and ready.

A cat came around the stairs and spotted him. He swore to himself, Stef hadn't mentioned a pet and winced as it mewed loudly, demanding attention. Distracted, he kicked at it as it ran past and burst into the front room. The curtains billowed as he saw the slender figure climbing out of the open window. Tomas grabbed a leg and pulled the person back inside. He recognised her as he wrapped an arm around her waist and she dropped her bag to fight him.

Perrette wriggled, sliding away and tried to get to the door. Tomas grabbed for her bodily, the only way to stop her attacking him. He twisted her to wrap his arms around her and pinned her own against her sides. Her head jerked back – he was expecting that and shifted. In return she jack-knifed her heels into his inner thigh.

"Don't do that," he roared, that was too close.

Unexpectedly she stopped, he'd probably deafened her. "Why?" She was still tense, she'd try something else if he dropped his guard.

"Because if you don't start behaving like a lady, I might have to stop behaving like a gentleman."

The huff of her ribs suggested she'd found his answer funny. "Gentlemen don't grab ladies, at least not where I come from, arsehole."

"Fine." He dragged her across to the table, slapped her face down, twisted both her wrists into one of his hands and looked around for something to tie them together with. There was a phone in the corner, he pulled the cable out of the socket, ignoring the clatter as it fell to the floor and wrapped it securely around her wrists, tying it tightly. "Now, sit and let's talk." He shoved her into a chair.

She smirked, "Enjoyed manhandling me did you?" Tomas glared and nearly smacked her. A hand snatched at him and pulled him round.

"What the hell do you think you're doing – that's Perri."

"What?" He nearly punched Stef instead, in no mood to give way. This woman had turned up one too many times.

"This is Chris' girlfriend, I've met her lots of times." Stef was looking from one to the other, Tomas could tell he was trying to think through the crap happening in his brain.

"Really? How long have you known her? She's not who you think she is."

"How long have you known me yourself?" Perrette was looking at Tomas. "How would you know anything. Stef, tell me you've not shacked up with this loser." Her chin went up at Tomas' glare. "Put him out Stef. Chris asked me to come here, he was worried about you, you weren't answering your phone."

"Shut up." She'd tricked him. If it hadn't been for her then he'd never have been waiting in that bar, would never have caught Stef's eye or had his bunker blown up in his face. The darker thought lurked that he would also have never had to share his god with another. He stuffed that thought down, not wanting to deal with it. The bar... "I was shot at in the bar the second time you turned up. You've spoken of other people wanting to find me, there was a man with you when I saw you at the train station." Perrette's eyes clouded for a moment and then cleared, she said nothing. "What does this Chris look like Stef? Is he tall and skinny with dark hair?"

"Yes." Stef's hand had dropped. The cat was rubbing around his legs and he absently picked it up as he walked over to shut the window and draw the curtains properly.

"Nearly every time I've seen you, you've been around another man – why?"

"Maybe I like the company." Her eyes flashed with anger.

Tomas' hand whipped out and took her by the throat. It was slender under his hand, he could feel the pulse beating. "Tell me why I shouldn't sacrifice you to my god," he whispered. His own heart was pounding, this woman had tricked him and yet she still had the body of the woman he'd loved for years, centuries. He could feel Al-Kiron rising behind him, her dark wings spreading and the rage igniting.

A weight threw itself on his arm, breaking the hold. Stef had him in a grip, his face white while Perrette bent over choking. "I won't let you do this to her. I tell you, she's Chris' girlfriend."

The rage was still rising, he could take Stef and then Perrette. They were both within touching distance and a moment would be all it would take. No more competition, no more dreaming of a woman who only existed in his imagination. Those barriers he'd put in place to protect himself were intensifying, he'd let them relax over the last few years, become soft. Once they were up he'd kill with impunity, not caring what the outcome was. He'd wait for this Chris and kill him too and then disappear.

A cold touch under his jaw, just where the blood flowed close to the surface and Tomas froze. Perrette was holding a knife to him, the only thing touching. "Kill Stef and you die." Her eyes were cold. Tomas released Stef and he slowly moved away. He now looked entirely sober and as though he was regretting sobriety bitterly. "I kill you and your god dies, it's the one thing we have in common. Back off Stef."

Ignoring Stef's gape, Tomas asked, "What do you mean?"

"You are Al-Kiron's last worshipper. I kill you and she crumbles."

Protect me… If he was her last worshipper then she would end up like those other gods he'd felt, the echoes coming out of the glades. The knife pressed a little harder and he closed his eyes. Was this going to be it? The knowledge that she wouldn't die was cold comfort, Stef couldn't protect himself from Perrette. He thought she was a friend and how long would it take for them to realise that Stef had her favour?

"Please take the knife away." Stef's voice was firm.

"You are not fucking serious Stef."

Tomas opened his eyes to see Stef pointing a gun at Perrette. Stef said, "If you hadn't pulled that thing then I might have believed you Perri. Move away from him."

"You can't stop me from killing him, I can make that thing malfunction."

"Can you stop me from killing you at the same time? There are two of us and only one of you." Tomas narrowed his eyes, "And what will happen to your god if you die?"

The blood drained out of Perrette's face. "You can't…"

Stef firmed his grip, "Try me."

There was none of the mirth left in his voice. Tomas admired the professional way he held the gun and tried to work out if he was actually bluffing or not. Perrette dropped her head and flipped the knife onto the table.

Tomas moved away in relief - that had been too close. "Well at least you believe me now. Perrette was the one to show me the Hall. I'd never been there before."

"You told him about the fucking Hall?"

Tomas answered before Stef could say he'd been there, "Of course, we're friends. How the fuck did you get your hands undone? I tied you up properly." A thought occurred to him, "And am I going to need to search you for more knives?"

"I always have a knife, even if it's not actually on me. It's a trick I can do, same as the wrists." She raised her chin, a spark of defiance in her eye, "Of course you can always try searching me, I'm sure you'd enjoy it."

"Do you want to search her Stef?"

Stef shook his head, "I've got the gun on her, between us both we can keep her contained."

"Just a warning that she can throw them too."

Perrette pulled a face at his words and said, "Your god must have been desperate."

"What do you mean?" He bristled at the thought he'd been taken on purely because there hadn't been anyone better around and it scratched against the childish part of him that hated her for taking Stef.

"They don't give away so much power unless they are." Tomas shook his head impatiently and she continued. "I'm a prime example, Dar gave me long life as well although my other tricks are only small. He's content with that, actually I've found most of the older gods tend to prefer staying inconspicuous."

"I don't have any tricks, I'm just trying to stay alive and sane."

"You can take a man's life by touching them, I'd say that's a pretty good trick."

Tomas flared, "Survival, if I don't then I'll die myself. Slowly and by degrees."

She laughed at that, "We're all dying, it's a human condition. Most people just have to deal with it." Her laughter sounded forced.

He narrowed his eyes, "You're hiding something, what are you protecting?" He almost jumped at his words. Protect me… the one thing they had in common. "You're Dar's last worshipper aren't you?"

"I can't say." Her lips were pressed together.

"I kill you and that's it, your god is dead." The feeling of power it gave him, he loomed over her.

"I can't say," she repeated.

"That's enough Tomas, back off." Stef's warning came from a distance. Tomas could feel Al-Kiron laughing, one touch and she would have a god's death… A metallic click inserted itself into his brain, he couldn't ignore it, he'd spent too many years in war zones. He flicked his eyes to the side, Stef had cocked the gun at him. “I told you to back off. Either of you make a wrong move and I’ll shoot.”

“You do know they’ll come for her don’t you?” Perrette licked her lips, watching them both nervously. A triangle linked them, none of them quite trusting enough to believe that any of them wouldn’t kill the other.

“What do you mean?” Tomas was only just holding back his rage, part of him couldn’t help calculating the steps it might take for him to get to Stef. Another, tinier part knew he’d be horrified by himself later.

“They know someone’s been using the Corridor, echoes have been felt in the outlying districts. They’ve got people working it out now.” She swallowed, “It won’t take long.”

Stef asked, “So, why are you in my house?”

Perrette looked as if she were in a bad dream, “I tell you and my god dies. He’s holding out, he’s held out for years. I don’t know how long I…”

Stef had the same compassionate look on his face as he’d had when Tomas had told him his story. “How can we help?” Tomas started to protest, she wasn’t to be trusted, she lied to him all these years. “Shut up.” Stef moved the gun ever so slightly towards him and he froze.

“I can’t. They got my god to stop me deliberately saying anything, I can only hint.”

“Convenient.”

Stef ignored Tomas’ dry remark, “Are you really Chris’ girlfriend?” Perrette stared at him, her body starting to shake. “Is Chris part of the problem?” Her shaking became stronger, her lips compressing. “Right, we deal with Chris first.”

Tomas asked sarcastically, “I thought Chris was your friend?”

“You’re right, I’m a sad bastard. I don’t actually trust anyone.” He looked at Tomas, his face grim. “I’ve been in this job for too long. We need to separate you from Chris first Perri."

"Hang on, first we need some answers to some questions. I want to know how long you've been hunting me for a start." Tomas was feeling increasingly marginalised.

"I can't say, don't you understand?" Perrette looked desperate.

"Tomas, will you ever learn to shut the fuck up?"

Tomas glared and was about to snap back at Stef when a bang at the front door interrupted him.

Chapter 12

They all froze at the noise, barely breathing, the triangle of not trusting welded into secrecy by the possibility of an intruder.

Stef looked at Perrette, "Is that Chris?" She didn't answer. "Will you betray us? If we can help you, we will." She shook her head violently and Tomas couldn't tell which question she was answering. The knock came again, a little louder.

"I need to go, I can't stay here." Perrette began wiping her face and straightening her clothes. In seconds she looked her normal self, only a tightness around her eyes betraying her feelings.

Stef nodded, "Looks like I came in as you were waiting for me, we had a really nice chat and we'll see each other again soon." His face was intent on hers and he tucked the gun into the back of his trousers, out of sight. Perrette smiled, the flicker of her old confidence igniting and Tomas felt the attraction pulling at him despite his ambivalence. He stepped back against the wall out of the way as Stef opened the front door to his so called friend and expressed his surprise at Perrette being there when he'd got back. The three of them laughed at Stef's embarrassed admission that he'd left his phone in the house that morning.

Perrette darted back into the room to get the bag she'd dropped, glanced up at him and pulled a face before ducking back into the hallway. Tomas found himself smiling back, his concern melting under the onslaught of memory. She'd always been deferential when he'd met her in the past, a woman had to be to survive. The flicker of mischief had attracted him but he'd never known her like this. Living in this century suited her, the confidence she had, the way she walked in the clothes that would have been a man's in the past. He'd given her the name Hephzibah and it suited her more than he'd known at the time.

He heard her airy comments in the hallway as she got ready to leave, Stef was giving his apologies for not offering them a drink, citing tiredness and a long day. Tomas flicked through all the times he'd seen Perrette, including the ones where she'd obviously not recognised him. His memories grew warmer at that time under the bridge, pulling her skirts up in a frantic coupling. She'd been as desperate as him. The front door slammed shut and Tomas wondered if she'd be interested in something a little more leisurely, they could have far more fun in these times. His smile deepened and he almost sauntered into the hall.

Stef ran his hands through his hair, "What are you smirking at?" He looked towards the door, concern on his face. "Fancy a coffee to talk all this through?"

"Haven't you got anything stronger? You might want to change your trousers first, you're still showing your arse."

He grinned as the other man swore in annoyance. "I'll get changed. There are glasses and drinks in the cupboard, sort yourself out."

Tomas paced the room with a whiskey, swirling the liquid as he walked. Perrette was with another man, possibly one that was controlling what she did. How could they leash her god like that? He wondered what he would do if his own was tethered and felt the rage. He kicked at one of the chairs and how much could he trust what she was saying?

"Mind the fucking furniture." Stef walked into the room and poured himself a whiskey. He put a saucer down, "Haven't got one of those smokes have you? I don't often indulge but I could do with one now."

Tomas passed him the packet and lit it for him. He sprawled in a chair, lighting his own and asked, "So, this Chris. Who is he?"

"He's my boss and I thought he was a friend."

"You've dropped him that quickly?"

"No. There's been a few things recently that I've not been happy about, Perri has actually been one of them. He's changed over the last few years." He stopped and swore.

"What?"

"I told Chris about my cabinet."

"And?"

Stef ignored him and ran out of the room and up the stairs. Tomas followed at a slower pace. He found the other man in the room above, facing the street. A desk took up most of the space and a few filing cabinets. One was open and Stef was rifling frantically through.

He slammed it shut. "It's gone." He sounded defeated.

"What's gone?"

"The USB stick with all my work on it." He looked embarrassed, "I had your movements on it for over fifty years. Some of it was patchy, there were some points where I didn't spot you for years but normally once I'd got hold of something, other things would crop up." Stef flung his hands up in the air, "Nothing left apart from a few printed photos."

"You'd been tracking me?"

"Passports, driving licences, contact details, the lot. All gone."

Tomas thought about where he'd been over the last fifty to a hundred years, all the way through Europe, following conflicts, always thinking ahead to what he might need in the future. The constant living his life on the edge, helping where he could and the horrors he'd seen from those less fortunate.

As though reading his mind, Stef said, "I had several documents from Eastern European orphanages marked as possible matches. Your features are unusual once you start looking at them and you've a predilection for getting papers in certain areas and for variations of your name." Stef mused, "Tomas is an easy name in a lot of ways. Put various squiggles on the letters and you can come from almost anywhere."

Tomas swore, he'd thought he'd been clever, obviously not clever enough. He'd been outed by a curious man with nothing else to do with his life. "And what does Chris have to do with this other than the fact that he was your friend?"

"He's the expert in this stuff. He encouraged me when I brought my findings to him…" Stef stopped talking, a horror spreading over his face. "What can he want from you?"

"Apart from wanting to kill me or my god? Fuck knows but I'm not going to stay here and find out. You got a rucksack? I need some shit and then I'm leaving."

"I'll get two, I'm coming with you."

Tomas swivelled round to look at him, "No way, you don't need to disappear."

"Wrong. What if these 'gods' favoured' find out about me? What if I have the same problems as you?"

"Then you have to deal with it, same as I did." Tomas was brutal.

"Listen to me, two heads are better than one and what about Perrette?"

"What about her?"

“Shouldn’t we do something about her situation? We could find out more from her, as she said, they’re looking to find Al-Kiron.”

Tomas squashed down the worry, “You’re not going all soft on Perrette are you? She can look after herself, she has so far. She’s centuries old, believe me I know.”

“Not when they’ve done something to her god and they’re looking to do the same to ours.”

Tomas blinked at Stef’s determination. He’d always held an ambivalence towards his god, an uneasy alliance. Stef’s surety despite having been attached to her for less than twenty four hours was unnerving. He himself hadn’t been like that for centuries, in fact the only time he’d been so grateful was when he’d been thanking her for saving his father’s life. To hear Stef also talking about her as their god made that part of him he didn’t want to think about twist inside.

“Do something yourself if you think you need to, don’t involve me.” He began to walk to the door and stopped at Stef’s next words.

“So that’s how you survived for so long, no one else matters apart from yourself. You were right, I am a sad bastard but at least I’m not a coward.” Tomas whirled around, and lashed his hand out, grabbing Stef’s arm. Stef went white but kept talking, refusing to back down. “Go for it. I intend to live my life not hide. I felt something out there when I knelt to Al-Kiron and I’m going to live up to it.”

Tomas felt an unfamiliar panic rising, life had been so simple up to this point. No one could judge him because no one had known him well enough or had been in his position. Now not only did he have people who were trying to kill him, there was also another man who was linked to his god. The twist inside tightened as he tried to see Stef as an ally not a competitor, it didn't work. People liked Stef. He was easy going and intelligent, qualities Tomas didn't feel he had in abundance.

Very few people had had the chance to know Tomas, he'd never let them. His life now stretched out, long and lonely. The chasm yawned between him and everyone else and he realised he needed friendship, simply having met Stef and told his story had created a bond between them. Had he been looking for that same ideal from all the times he'd sought out Perrette? An unconscious wanting to share the burden of his long life?

Stef was still staring at Tomas, breathing heavily. "Well, are you going to kill me?"

Tomas let go and said gruffly, "Give me some fucking credit." He turned to walk out of the door, "I want to finish my whiskey. Let's talk while I do."

Stef chuckled, "You don't like backing down do you? Have you thought that maybe that's why she chose you?"

"What?" Tomas jerked around again, staring.

"All that time you spent asking for help when you were a young boy, you didn't give in. Maybe she knew you wouldn't just turn up your toes at the first challenge. Then you've survived all this time on your own, that actually takes guts."

"I thought you said I was a coward. I'm frightened of dying." He grated the words out, hating the sound of them.

"I think we're all frightened of dying, that's not actually being a coward. Refusing to help someone when you can, now that's different."

Stef's eyes assessed him, he'd not felt this naked for years. Could he actually have helped Perrette all that time ago? How long had her god been trapped? He tried to tell himself that he hadn't known and knew that he'd also not given her the time to ask. All those times he'd seen her, not realising her predicament or her likeness to himself.

He turned away, not wanting to see his reflection in Stef's eyes. "I need my whiskey," he repeated. Stef snorted and gestured for them to walk down the stairs. They sat and Stef re-filled their glasses.

Tomas found his cigarette burnt to ashes in the saucer and lit another, pausing his thoughts while the smoke coiled through his lungs. "So Mr Detective, we're in your sphere of expertise. I'm just the grunt here, what's the plan?"

"I'd like to go and confront Chris, however I'm not sure what impact that would have on Perri. We can't leave her with him once he realises we know."

"So?"

"I'd say let's go for her god, if we can free him then maybe he'll be able to extract her."

"You do know it doesn't work like that don't you? Gods don't just wave their hands and sort out our problems, they expect us to do the heavy lifting."

"Maybe I'm being idealistic about this. If we get Perri out first then they'll go for her god. What happens if someone's god dies?"

"No idea. She didn't seem happy about it though."

Stef snorted, "We can guess it's probably not nice. How do we find a god in the Hall?"

So many questions they didn't know the answers to. "I'm not sure, apparently they move around. You interviewed me in the hospital, did you find out who was shooting at me or the name of the man who died?"

"No, Chris…" Stef paused, "Chris took over the investigation. He said they'd had an anonymous warning, I'm starting to disbelieve that now."

Tomas swore, he was beginning to hate that man. “He’s your boss, will there be any notes? They might lead us somewhere.”

“There may be something on the system, but I can’t access that from here.” Stef put down his glass firmly, “I’ll get my keys.”

Chapter 13

The office was scruffy, the paint peeling from the top of the room. Bits of paper covered the desk, overflowing from the trays. Stef had driven them, using his status to get Tomas into the building without any questions. He'd also refused to rush after getting his keys, insisting on enjoying a fresh cigarette first despite Tomas' impatience to find out what the police had on him.

Tomas looked around, "This is one of the perks for a stressful job? You've been had, I'd find another career if this is what I'd got."

"Piss off, I've got a window - unlike most people here."

He snorted, "I've been building places like this for decades, nice to see they're looked after."

Stef ignored the sarcasm and started the computer up. Tomas stared out of the window. They were high up in the building, a splatter of rain beating against the glass. Down below was the road with a few cars parked along it, beyond that were the neon streetlights and the moody river. He rarely stared out of windows in the dark and avoided most mirrors, the chance of seeing her was something he tended to avoid. Not this time, he could feel himself reaching out. Was this the right thing to do? Helping another's god felt an anathema to him. She was far away, was this a sign of her distaste? He remembered his words to Stef about gods expecting you to help yourself and sighed.

Below him, two figures came out of the main entrance, one slightly in front of the other. He craned slightly, curious about who was out at this time of night and then drew back as far as he could. "Stef."

Stef was thumping the keys, "Hang on… What's up?"

"What does Chris look like again?"

"Tall, skinny chap. Why?"

"Would you recognise him from above?"

Stef muttered a swear word and came over. He blinked and swore further, "Yes, that's him, how did you guess?"

"Perrette's over there by that car." There was no mistaking her slender figure encased in the leather coat. Tomas flicked the office light off and they stood closer to the window. The taller figure was waving his arms as Perrette folded hers, leaning against the car door.

"We could go down and get her now."

"That's not the detective thinking, that's your boss down there arguing with his girlfriend. No one will see anything else." They watched as the taller of the two got into the car and slammed the door shut. Perrette stayed leaning for a few seconds and then got in. "So, they were here. I wonder why?"

"Fuck knows. Let's find out what's happened to this case." Tomas came to peer over Stef's shoulder as he worked. "You're not actually supposed to see this."

"I'm not supposed to be in the building and yet you wangled me in."

Stef tapped a few more keys and a screen came up. "I don't actually believe it."

"What?" Tomas tried to make sense of the report and the messages coming up.

"He's closed it." Stef flicked through several pages. "He's actually attempted to bury it under other stuff. No recommendations to look for the gun man, only if 'sufficient resources are available'. Bollocks, there are never enough resources. There's a report on the dead man, died of sepsis, no other investigation needed. No report needed on the officer having shot him either, it's considered 'reasonable force considering the circumstances'. How the hell did he think I'd accept it?" He slammed a hand down on the papers covering the desk.

"Does he need you to?"

Stef snorted, "I'd have asked him about it."

"And the man in my flat?"

"Chris…" Stef stopped himself.

"Chris arranged it. There'll be an explanation for that one too then." Tomas' voice was flat. This Chris was getting too involved for his liking. He fancied having a long conversation with him, preferably one with his hand around his throat.

"That man in the bar, he was close to you from the reports I read. Why didn't you just…" Stef mimed holding someone and then waved his hand.

"I tried, she wouldn't let me do it." The feeling of the hand rising under his, then the explosion and the sudden pain. Stef's face was full of speculation. "What?"

He mused, "Imagine if people knew we had someone like you on the force, we'd have a far easier time bringing them in. We could just threaten them and they'd give up."

Tomas was horrified. "You don't seem to understand, this isn't something I can control, I have to do this to stay sane." He couldn't explain the difficulties of trying to stay the same age to keep his mind balanced, of keeping himself in one piece while the world changed around him. It had become harder over the last century or so, the years seeming to gallop by and bringing new challenges to face.

"Then why not use the bad people in the world? Those in prison, wouldn't that make it easier?"

Tomas hesitated, he'd struggled with this for centuries. "Because I am not a god, I can't judge people like that." He could only take at face value. Life was so precious, could he really allow himself to be used in that way? He imagined walking into a cell block knowing the man inside would die and shied away, it was bad enough with some random killer in war zones or an unfortunate in an alleyway. He said softly, "I am very much a man."

Stef laughed, "That's why I like you, no grandeur about your abilities." Tomas blinked, Stef liked him? His mind flipped back to their ease when they'd met at Stef's flat and his assertion to Al-Kiron that Stef was his friend in the glade. He'd not actually thought it through and a warmth spread, for the first time he actually had an ally.

"What's this?" Stef had gone back to his desk to look further at the files and shifted the paperwork under his hand to uncover a USB stick. "I didn't leave this here," he said softly. He plugged it in and opened the files. "This is my USB from home."

"You couldn't have left it here by accident?" Tomas was itching to see what Stef had on him, in the knowledge that Chris also now had that information. He needed to know which of his fake identities had been compromised.

"No, I normally email anything to Chris, but he did know about it."

Another thought intruded and Tomas said, "Perrette's been in here then."

"Maybe she left it here."

"At who's order?"

"You're a suspicious bastard."

"It's what's kept me alive. She nearly had me arrested by the town bailiffs once, before I knew who she was."

Stef grinned, "Go her."

"Not really, I thought my performance had been better than that."

Stef nearly fell off his chair laughing at the dry comment. "Have you really met her before?"

"I thought I was meeting someone who looked like her." The old hurt pulled. The stolen glances at a woman across a room, leaving before they could form any kind of attachment and stop the heartache that he'd have to see her grow old. He clenched his fists, none of that had been necessary. "She's a very good actress. I don't trust her."

"But there's an attraction."

Tomas shrugged, deflecting the question, "I suppose she's my type." He stopped and glowered at Stef, "You don't fancy her do you?"

"Nah, I prefer short cuddly blondes myself." The other man mimed wrapping his arms around a large figure. "I like something comfortable in bed."

"Stef, did you tell Chris you'd found me?"

"Yes."

"And that you'd given me your number?"

"Yes." The repeated word was harder. "That's why I don't consider him to be a friend now. I realised that he'd sent those men after us at my flat. No one else knows about it apart from Chris. He'd guess I'd see you there."

"Arsehole."

"Precisely. Which means that this has been planted." He pinged the USB stick with a finger. "Do you think he's one of these gods' favoured?"

"Let's assume for the moment he is, what advantage does he have by putting that thing on your desk where you'll find it?"

"I normally come in first thing and tidy my desk, it's a habit of mine to start the day. He used to wind me up that I left it in a mess every evening."

"So someone knew you'd find it in the morning."

"Yes." Stef leaned on his elbow, staring at the screen. "Wait, what's this?" Tomas peered over his shoulder. "Look, it's another file, I've not seen this one before."

"What's it called?"

"The Hall of Antiquities."

"That file says read me. Open it."

Stef clicked on the document and it opened.

"Hello Stef,

"You've probably worked out that your new friend Tomas is a very interesting man and not just because you have been chasing him through the years. He is the last true worshipper of a god called Al-Kiron. This isn't to say he's the only one like himself, there are thousands of gods with only one or two worshippers and they infest the Hall like rats. The gods' favoured have dedicated themselves to ridding the Hall of this vermin.

"The difference between these vermin and Tomas is that his god gave him a large amount of herself when they made their bargain. Most such favoured mortals only get the chance to see their god's face and the ability to step into the Hall. Tomas has been given far more.

"What do the gods gain by giving us these things? For a start the level of belief becomes far higher, the priests who have never stepped foot in the Hall are subject to a blind faith and devotion most can't sustain long term. Why do you think religion and faith bring war? The gods require the passion given out, they are emotional vampires and they grow stronger through feeding off it.

"It also takes energy for a god to appear even partially in this world and most die slowly if they can't muster enough to bring someone through. The Hall itself has its own quirks, the Corridor is the only safe route through it. The dangers of the cribbet are minor compared to those of the gods desperate for worshippers in their last dying throes and the chances of falling through the landscape.

"The larger gods huddle together, drawn by the gravity of belief and it solidifies the landscape. Further out along the Hall, the minor gods stretch out into eternity. There are theories that the Hall spans not only this world but other worlds as well, still more suggest that there may be a way to bend time itself if the Hall is used in the correct way. The gods remain silent on both those aspects.

"Still, no one has ever walked the entire length of the Hall, indeed, anyone who has tried has never returned. We have a map of how the major gods move across the Corridor, a crude thing. They are constrained by their own laws, one moving will change where the others lie and it's possible to work out where others are from that. Some shift almost nightly, with others it depends on the phase of the moon or tides.

"How does this all affect you Stef? I would ask you to tell your friend that I'm waiting for him. We had thought his god dead, supplanted by others. Both he and Al-Kiron have hidden for too long. Tell him that I have our people working our maps, checking the oscillations of the Corridor and we will find her soon. We will cut her off and force him to us. If he surrenders then we will allow him to live, if not then they will both die.

"I look forward to meeting him in person, Chris."

Tomas stared at the screen, "Arsehole."

"Do you think he got recruited by someone? "He never used to be like this." Stef mused, "He's right about the being overwhelmed though, I had it with Al-Kiron."

"Do you regret it?"

Stef shrugged, “For me it’s brought a completion, I imagine for others it’s different. Chris has been angry for several years, I wonder if this is why.”

“That I can understand.”

“Why do you think he’s taking his anger out on others? What’s in it for him?”

“A bully gets to see those smaller than himself suffering more.” Tomas wasn’t so interested in the reasons, “We need to work out what we’re doing next.”

“Let’s look at the other file.”

It proved to be a complex diagram with overlapping circles and arrows with numbers and letters above them.

“What the fuck?” Tomas couldn’t make head or tail of it.

“This must be the map he was talking about. Look, there’s tomorrow’s date on it. The arrows must be the direction they’ll travel in.”

“And the size of the circles?”

Stef shrugged, “Maybe that’s the size of the gods. There are so bloody many of them.”

“What’s on the next page?” Tomas was fascinated despite himself.

“The date is for the day after tomorrow, these two circles have moved, that one hasn’t.”

Tomas watched Stef running his finger across the screen and felt irritable at the complexity. “It changes every day?”

“There’s about a week’s worth here. These pluses and minuses become larger every day. They mustn’t be able to predict that far into the future.”

He nodded sharply, “Chris knows we’re connected now, this was deliberate. It won’t be long before he finds out that you’ve become favoured as well. He can’t get rid of me here, there are too many bodies piling up around this case. He can’t cover all of them up, someone will notice eventually. If he can blame you then he will but I think he'd rather do it where it doesn't matter. It would be more convenient for me to simply disappear."

"So we do something he's not expecting?"

"Yes. You were right earlier." Tomas smiled briefly at Stef's surprise and took the USB stick out. The screen went blank as he pocketed it. "He's going to expect me either to run or to confront him. I'm not doing either. We're going after Dar."

What's changed your mind?"

"Perrette knows more about the Hall than I do, we need her knowledge before we try anything else and besides," Tomas paused for effect. "I love a grateful woman."

Stef snorted, "Bastard."

Tomas chuckled and waved Stef out with an exaggerated gesture.

Chapter 14

"Okay, so from what I understand they won't be able to tell if we've arrived in a busy part of the Corridor. It's only when someone enters on the edges that they'll notice as it's more unusual."

"Sounds like a giant lilo."

"A what?" Tomas generally felt he did well keeping up with the times, but there were occasions when he got knocked off track by a word he didn't immediately recognise.

Stef laughed at his look, "A vast inflatable floating on water. You jump on one end and the whole thing moves."

Tomas grunted, speaking several languages didn't help either, he couldn't keep up with all the colloquialisms in all of them. They'd stopped off at a small pub to eat close to Stef's house. The number of people felt reassuring and the music a comfortable din, normal life playing around them. The thought of someone coming in with a weapon seemed far away despite Tomas's hospital stay being less than two weeks ago.

Stef continued, "I can't believe there's a whole other world out there and we're going to storm it."

"Welcome to my life."

"Even you didn't know this, doesn't it excite you?"

Tomas sighed, "No. I like my world staying boring and simple. I've worked on building sites for the last three years as a labourer here. No one trying to kill me is exciting. The occasional woman coming my way with a smile and more. Good food and a drink or two." He raised his pint to Stef and drank.

"You'd have been happy all those years ago if your father had simply recovered and you'd lived making bowls?" They leaned back to let the barman put food in front of them.

"Yes. It was all I wanted." Tomas took a bite and chewed. "I realise now that he wasn't old, he was in his thirties at the most. People, especially people of our status didn't live long then but I would have been content because that's all I knew."

"But all the stuff you've seen over the years, all the inventions?"

Tomas chuckled, shaking his head, "Every time I see something good invented, it's used in a twisted way. I keep hoping but the human race doesn't appear to learn. It's fundamentally selfish. Admit it, you're a detective, you see the seamy side of life as part of your day job. The bad guys keep finding new ways to slip through your nets and keep doing what they want to."

"Maybe this sad bastard wants to keep hoping that things will get better."

They both chuckled, the crowded room feeling cosy. Tomas felt more relaxed than he had for years in someone else's company. The usual worry of being noticed, of someone spotting something different about him didn't apply with Stef. They'd the shared experience of the Hall and their god. He'd have to watch Stef grow old, he doubted she'd given Stef the same as him but for some reason that didn't bother him. The twist of jealousy eased and he smiled while he ate. The assertion he'd made to his god that Stef was a friend felt right.

"What's up?"

Tomas shook his head, "Just thinking that I've a friend and I quite like it."

"And you're calling me the sad bastard." Stef laughed and tilted his own glass, "Cheers, here's to sad bastards everywhere." They finished their meal and lingered over the drinks. "So, we have a plan?"

Tomas said, "We need weapons that will survive the transfer which means nothing modern and we need to work out that map."

"I have various things back at the house we can use. Failing that, I have kitchen knives."

"We could throw your cat at them?"

"Piss off, Moppet's not to be used gratuitously."

"Moppet?" He snorted, "You have got to be kidding me."

"It's the name she came with," Stef sniffed.

"Name? The only thing cats care about is the tin opener. You may as well call it…" Tomas started making the sound of a tin lid coming off.

Stef stood, "I'm going for a piss before we fall out." He tried to glare and failed.

"Over your cat?" Tomas chuckled and settled down to finish his drink as Stef went to find the toilet. They'd find a way of stopping Chris discovering Al-Kiron. Perrette was the key to more information, apart from that he wanted to continue the conversation they'd started in the hospital. The teasing warmth in her eyes, promising more. He smiled to himself, somehow he'd find a way to make that warmth a reality again. That single time with her so many years ago, there had been other women before and after but none with the same intensity.

The good feeling faded as a twist ran through his stomach, Stef had said Chris was her boyfriend. Was that only for convenience or was that something else? Her body language had certainly suggested she wasn't with him willingly tonight. That time in the hospital, had that been at Chris' insistence? Would she have actually slept with him just so he could be caught? Despite his teasing over wanting a grateful woman, his own instincts were matching Stef's here, willing was one thing, coerced was another. His thoughts plummeted further, what if that time under the bridge had been similar?

He let the noise of the pub wash over him and raised his glass to take the last gulp and frowned. Stef had taken longer than he'd realised. He stretched, looking through the people and saw another man push through the toilet door on the other side of the room. Tomas began to stand, thinking he'd go and check.

A shout and the man who'd just walked through the door backed out. Tomas muttered a swear word and pushed his way closer, not sure what he'd see. A flurry of noise and a cold began to rise from the pit of Tomas' stomach. He glanced towards the mirror, for once wanting her to appear in its depths and tell him whether to run or not. He squashed the automatic impulse, he had to know where Stef was. The mirror remained frustratingly normal, reflecting the outside world not his inner one amid the black lines of alcoholic advertising. He switched his attention to those around him. A barman was trying to keep people away from the now open door.

Tomas peered over people's shoulders to see a strange man lying on the floor with a head wound. The inner door to the toilet was open and there was no sign of Stef. He swore, noticing another barman was talking on his mobile. He picked out snatches of conversation, someone mentioned Stef or rather described him. The pieces of information were linked like a puzzle, others chiming in that he'd been sitting with another man. It had been noticed that Stef had gone in and most would assume that the man had been attacked by him and that they'd missed Stef coming out again, there was only a tiny window, far too small for a man of Stef's build to get through.

People turned to look at Tomas and he twitched, disliking being the centre of attention. A man asked him if he'd seen his friend and he shrugged, making a loud comment that he'd left a few minutes ago. He saw the barman waving at him to stay and ducked his head, pretending not to see him - there was no way he was staying here to be questioned.

Tomas used the confusion to slide out of the pub and heard the wail of an ambulance coming down the street. That was fast. There was no way out of the toilet without using the door. That twist he'd felt, had someone taken Stef through rather than his thoughts causing it? Perrette had described something as generating shocks, had this been the same? Tomas glared as he walked and people around him cleared out of his path in the cool night air. His fists clenched, Chris must be getting desperate to kidnap Stef.

Stef had said that he had weapons that could be used at his house, he'd go back there and decide what he was doing next. The key in his pocket, he'd wound Stef up about giving it away to anyone and Tomas had shut up when he'd looked sad and said only to friends.

Ignoring the cold and the late night revellers, Tomas walked several miles swiftly into the street were Stef lived. He checked the length, not trusting that Chris wouldn't have spies. He walked on edge, every parked car was a potential ambush in the neon light and spotted nothing. All was quiet, a suburban street in London, family life going on behind the closed doors and drawn curtains. The house was empty apart from Moppet running up to him. Tomas absently picked the cat up and it purred into his ear.

"You should be out hunting mice fleabag," he muttered.

He began to ransack the rooms, looking for a rucksack, food and anything else he could take. The cat ran into the open cupboards, refusing to come out until he'd opened another, making him swear. The house was going to look like it had been burgled at this rate. He found a radio and put it on for company.

The gun Stef had used was back in its locked drawer in the hall, Tomas rattled the lock and left it there. He needed something simpler – he couldn't take it with him. He found a couple of heavy knives he liked the look of but he wanted a weapon with a bit more reach. A modern looking bow tempted him until he realised he didn't know how accurate he could be with it. In Stef's office he found a longer knife left on a shelf. He hefted it, feeling for its balancing point and decided it would work for the moment but it needed sharpening. At close quarters he had only to touch someone, with this as well he'd do fine.

He walked back down the stairs and started to hone it on a knife stone Stef had in his kitchen drawer and suddenly tuned into the news report on the radio. "A man has been found injured in a pub in Kingston. Police are saying that fingerprints on the weapon found at the scene match those of a Tomislav Horvat, recently thought to have been involved in another incident."

What the fuck? He'd not been anywhere near the toilet until the man had been found. Was this Chris' work? This would make it far harder for him to move around. Tomas switched on the tv and saw a picture of himself flashing up after the news reel at the pub toilets. The scene switched to that of the other bar, the news reader said that new evidence had come out to suggest that he may have been responsible for the deaths instead of being the hero. The public were being told not to approach him as he might be dangerous. Tomas swore, Chris was losing no time in using anything he could. The fact that he'd been sitting ten feet away in plain view made no difference. The general public thought he was guilty and would be looking for him.

His stomach drew tighter as footage from the bus station's camera was used, suggesting that he was able to disguise his age. No dark haired, olive skinned man would be safe in London, everyone would be scrutinised. He squashed the urge to disappear, Chris would use his position to accuse him of all sorts until he was cornered. Every incident they could would be pinned on him. He had to act now and move in a direction they wouldn't be expecting, especially as he didn't know how far Chris would go to make Stef talk. His mind shuddered away from the brutalities he'd seen in war.

He pulled the USB stick out of his pocket, absently flipping it while he thought. If he remembered rightly, the way markers were at roughly even distances between the various gods. There'd not been any names on the map, just numbers. He tossed it onto the table and watched as Moppet jumped up and began to play with it.

Tomas switched the light off and stared into the mirror above the fireplace, reaching out. Slowly the image formed behind him, the cold cheek contrasting with the warm light in the hallway. Her dark eyes opened.

"Please help me," Tomas whispered.

The reply was a breath of wind from a graveyard. "You are the important one my Tomas, he is a sacrifice. Run while you can, save us both."

"No. They are looking for you too. You need both of us."

"So stubborn, not so long ago you would have fought to stay alone. If you run then they will never find me and I can cut the other's tie."

A horror spread through him, was that all that was keeping him alive? If she chose to cut his tie, what would happen to him? While Stef was still attached to her, she could find him. Stef hadn't asked to get caught up in all this, he'd made Tomas feel more connected to life than he had for years. Stef was his friend. "No. I need him, even if I watch him die of old age eventually, I need him."

"I cannot help you with this, any movement on my part will lead them to me. I risk detection even by speaking to you, they are coming. I must leave you to your fate then my Tomas. Run while you can."

He reached out for her, wanting her to take him to the Hall. Too late, the crescent of cold light faded and Tomas was left gasping in rage. She wouldn't help him, she wanted him to run. He clenched his fists and shouted at the glimmer left, "You cut that tie to Stef and I'll fucking kill myself."

Nothing answered. The feeble threat echoed in his ears, they both knew he wouldn't. Tomas stood panting and stared at the cat. She'd tapped the USB stick to the edge of the table and was looking at him. Not wanting to pick it up off the floor he said, "Don't do that."

A paw stole out and still watching him, she flicked it off. He narrowed his eyes, he couldn't even get a fucking cat to behave. There was a flash of car lights outside as he picked the stick up and he peered through a gap in the curtains and swore again. She'd been right, they were gathering and he had no time to plan further. Tomas looked through a back window and saw torch light bobbing – they'd try and block off both entrances at once. Chris was pushing his hand, he'd have to act.

All of a sudden Tomas smiled, "Thank you Moppet." He reached out to rub the cat's ears and she stretched against him. He was bigger and stronger than her and yet she'd still made him pick the USB stick up off the floor. He could do the same to Al-Kiron, if the police got hold of him then he'd be put into Chris' hands and she didn't want that.

Someone had a loudhailer and was asking him to come out with his hands up. He wondered if Chris was waiting out there, somewhere far back so he couldn't get hurt or maybe he was interrogating Stef. Tomas clenched his fists, taking a deep breath, this was going to hurt. He slung his coat on and picked up the knife. Standing in the hall he could see in both directions, they were waiting at both ends and he readied himself. It was quiet outside now, he flicked the lights off, allowing his eyes to adjust. He could feel his heart thudding and continued his deep breathing, pulling the oxygen into his muscles, waiting for that moment when everything would happen.

As the front door burst open, he drew the knife and deliberately ran at them, bellowing defiance and reached out to her at the same time. The first baton descended and he wondered if he'd miscalculated.

Chapter 15

Tomas lay on the damp ground and groaned. She'd not spared him any pain and he hurt all over. He'd charged into the mass of men coming into the hallway and butted the first in the stomach with the reverse of his knife. The man had folded beautifully. After that it had been close quarter fighting, he'd kept hold of the knife in one hand and reached out to touch others, sending them to Al-Kiron with a grim determination.

To his surprise, he'd nearly got out although he'd received his own fair share of bruises. These men couldn't have known what they were dealing with, certainly there hadn't been any of the gods' favoured amongst them. It had been the second wave coming through the rear of the house that had forced him back and just at the point of him being overwhelmed, Al-Kiron had taken him through.

A hand flopped from his arm and he looked over to see the body he'd brought with him. Tomas sighed, he was only young. With no obvious cause of death, he looked as though he'd taken an unexpected nap. He tucked his knife away. It was all he had, no rucksack, no supplies and no plan apart from the idea of finding Dar or Stef. He didn't even know where he was.

With one last look at the man lying at his feet, Tomas began to test the ground and walk towards the Corridor. The noise she'd made pulling him through, he felt deafened although he could still hear the strange sounds of the woods. He needed to get away from this area as quickly as possible. She'd taken away the years he'd gained from the deaths when he'd transferred, he could feel the difference in his stride.

Something made him freeze, all his senses were on edge here and these woods were pinging every one of his nerves honed from the battlefield. Slowly he dipped down to the ground, thankful his clothes were dark. A howl, almost human pierced the gloom close and a shiver ran over his skin. Creeping forwards, he wondered what else this strange place could throw at him.

A figure stood close to the track leading to the corridor swinging his head. He was dressed normally in jeans and a jumper apart from the knee length cloak he wore. He flipped the hood of his cloak up and down, clutching a staff to him as he peered around. He was as young as the body Tomas had left on the ground behind him but this was no police officer. He was broadcasting his presence, flattening himself to a tree and trying to keep an eye everywhere at once. The cry sounded out again and he spun around searching for the source, Tomas could almost smell his fear.

Tomas stayed calm, he was a hunter, not the hunted. He collected himself and drew his knife, it now looked short in the half light. A gasp from the other man made him jerk his head up. He watched as he pulled his cloak off and threw it away, gripping the staff hard between shaking hands. Tomas could only the shadow of a figure between the trees. The mournful cry sounded again much closer.

"Go away." The other man's voice cracked and Tomas wondered what could be frightening him so much. He shifted, intending to allow these two assailants to pick each other off when the figure in the trees raced forward at a frightening speed, one hand dipping down to touch the ground as it ran. With a shriek, the man lashed out with one end of the staff and it connected with a meaty smack. Tomas silently applauded the strike and gaped when the figure didn't appear to notice. The figure grasped the staff and pulled it out of the man's hand, ignoring how the other attempted to keep hold of it and threw it onto the ground. The man stumbled, turning his back as he tried to run, his mouth gaping in terror.

Fuck that, Tomas was no longer a spectator in this game and didn't care that he'd killed enough today. No longer caring that the other man might be an enemy, he got ready to run forwards, hand outstretched and then paused, fear drenching him as the figure finally came into the light, intent on its victim. It spotted Tomas and stared, distracted between the two targets. Tomas stared back, frozen at the skull-like face, its nostrils shrivelled back into two gaping holes and the mouth full of long teeth. It was smaller than he was and dressed in ragged clothes, a parody of humanity. As he stared, the younger man scrambled to his feet and the creature's attention switched back. It shifted so fast he barely saw it move, reaching out to grasp an arm and casually ripped out the man's spine.

Tomas couldn't move, all his experience had been for human conflicts even face to face and looking into another man's eyes. He'd never dealt with anything like this almost human thing, snarling over what was increasingly a pile of meat. He took a step back, hoping to get away while it was busy and its head jerked up at the movement, blood dripping from its mouth and hands.

He swore internally as the corpse was dropped, an unwanted toy. The creature snarled and flung itself at him, frighteningly fast, a howl moaning from deep in its chest. He stared into the black pits of its eyes, knowing he'd have one chance. It brushed his knife aside - the power in that hand despite its size. Its nails scraped his wrist and the stench of its body up close was incredible, what the fuck was it?

Survival took over, his own hand raised and the black light flashed out as his god took it. The body dropped next to that of the man it had killed, he swore he could see a smile on its lips. He panted, the aftermath of adrenalin running through him from the fights in both worlds. He waited, everything tingling and conscious of this strange place, ready for any more attacks from the dark woods.

Whoops and shrieks came periodically, nothing more than when he'd been with Perrette. Slowly his breathing returned to normal and he studied the corpse at his feet. With the deep set eyes now closed, the face looked almost human but nothing could survive with so little on its bones. It was grey with ingrained dirt and splattered with blood from the man it had dismembered. His gaze travelled down further and he jumped back, bile gathering in his throat. It was female, a sagging tit hung out of the scraps of clothing covering it.

Tomas remembered the vision Al-Kiron had shown him of Stef changing, the flesh hanging off him and clothed in tatters. Had this once been human? He shook his head, what could have made a woman into this monster? Shuddering he became aware of his hand, aching in the aftermath of the fight. Its nails had scratched his wrist, he twisted it absently knowing he'd need to bathe it when he came across some water. He briefly thought of his god's pool and smiled at the sacrilegious idea of washing the blood away there.

His foot scuffed against something and he nearly shouted, unnerved by the dead creature in front of him. It was the cloak that had been discarded, Tomas picked it up, he'd not worn a cloak for years. He hesitated, wanting to cover the dead bodies and yet the weight of the fabric pulled at him. Almost furtively he slung it around his shoulders and it settled on him in folds he recognised from childhood onwards. He pulled the hood up and suddenly remembered doing the same on his way to find his god the first time, although that cloak had only been hip length and threadbare.

He flipped the hood back down and decided to keep it purely for nostalgia despite enjoying the practicalities of modern dress. Zips and tailoring, even buttons made clothing so much nicer. His knife was on the floor where he'd dropped it and he silently apologised to both of the bodies as he stuck it back in his belt.

Tomas suddenly remembered the staff the young man had been holding and found it in the bushes a little way away. It looked as though it was stained black in the uncertain light and it was covered in carvings. The patterns appeared a little out of line with each other, he twisted them and found it unscrewed into three parts. He grunted in approval at the useful adaption for when the owner would be carrying it in the real world and tightened them to make them match up the best he could. He hefted it, found it a good weight and smiled - he'd found the weapon he was after.

Shrugging off the nagging guilt that he should do something about the corpses, he found the track and began walking. The ground was more stable here, from what Perrette had said this should mean it was a well-travelled area. He couldn't wait for anyone to turn up looking for the dead man. The noises continued as before and he kept a wary eye out for any movement. He slowed as he came to the Corridor and stayed out of sight, watching for a while. There were flickering figures moving on it and some slower, walking at a normal pace. Those moving faster appeared to be passing through the others. He shivered, this place was strange.

He stared in curiosity, most people appeared to be cloaked similar to himself and some wore visible weapons, nothing was modern in appearance. He pulled his hood over his face and was just about to step on when a stronger shiver went through him and he stepped away. Those walking slowly on the Corridor also stepped to one side and onto the grass verges. Tomas peered from underneath his hood, trying not to look as though he was panicking. He'd be noticed if he moved away, most people were looking in one direction and waiting impatiently, commenting to their neighbours. There was a movement in the distance.

"Fucking Degenerated." Tomas flicked a look at the man who'd stopped next to him and grunted in response. He had no idea what the man was talking about. The figures coming towards them this time were slower and more substantial, although they were still moving faster than those who'd been walking. As they drew closer, he had to stop himself from stepping back further.

The creatures being herded along the Corridor were the same as had attacked the man at the way marker. He stayed in place purely by force of will, his wrist tingled and his fingers itched to scratch it. They moaned and swiped as they ran, kept in place by men with whips. So many of them, his mind shuddered away from the idea that they might have once been human.

"Money's a bastard god if you ask me." The man spat to the side. "And it's getting worse with them using those things."

Tomas risked, "I'm a bit new here, what do they use them for?"

The man laughed nastily, "Haven't you heard? They use them to block a weak god's power. When your god's got no access then they're helpless and if they bring enough then they can kill it. I've even heard rumours that they've brought the Baron out from confinement and that's bad."

Tomas daren't ask any more questions, they were working out were Al-Kiron was and would surround her with those things. A rage grew at the thought of her unable to access him despite his hatred of what he did to stay alive. It was a bargain between them both, others shouldn't get involved.

"Whose god is yours?" The question came casually.

Tomas twisted a smile and said, "One who doesn't want certain visitors calling." He nodded towards the chaos in front of them.

The man nodded, "None of us want visitors like that calling, we've all been walking on tenterhooks since they discovered how to herd those things."

He took a risk, "I hear they have a map too."

"It's the most accurate map there is around here and I bet you can guess what they use it for. They keep a rough copy at the temple for people to look at but the complete one is back in the real world, so no one knows where they are to garotte them for it."

They shared an understanding smile. "So where were they going, just so I don't bump into them? I'm new in this area." Tomas guessed from Perrette's earlier words that most people didn't know much about the Hall outside their own range.

"You really are a country boy." The insult was said without any heat behind it. "The Degenerated looked stuffed so they'd be coming back from mucking around with some unfortunate bastard. They'd be having a far harder time handling them otherwise. The major gods hold the central area stable enough for them to have their own marker instead of the usual stones. Look for the one with the columns, that's Money's. It'll be busier around there too. A bit of advice, keep your head down while you're around that area and if anyone challenges you then lick the floor if that's what they ask." At Tomas' look he clarified, "Some of them can follow your trail back to your god and you don't want that if your god has under a certain number of followers."

The mess of degenerated humanity had disappeared up the Corridor and people were relaxing and stepping back onto the road. The man waved his thanks away and stepped onto the Corridor and flickered out. Tomas forced himself to breathe, thinking through his options while he watched the figures. He wanted to find Stef and get out of here. If what that man had said was true then they'd be able to use Stef to find Al-Kiron. He swore to himself, he still didn't know enough about this place. If he was in a war zone somewhere then this would be easy. Sneaking around, that was what he was good at.

The realisation hit him and he nearly groaned in his mindset not being flexible enough - this was a war zone, despite the difference in landscapes. He would be captured and possibly killed if he was found. Sneaking it was then, to find out the information he needed. Tomas flipped his hood up and stepped onto the Corridor. He walked, stubbornly ignoring those who appeared to be coming at him at high speed and concentrated on his feet. He found himself reaching out as he walked. Al-Kiron was a long way behind him, here there were no dead or broken gods only the small white stones proclaiming those minor. Ahead of him was a curious weightiness, a solidity. He could feel the Corridor almost dipping and pulling him towards it. Without thinking, Tomas reached out mentally and grasped. He found the landscape blurring, people rushing towards him and disappearing before they hit. He had to remind himself to breathe, his first impression of the Corridor hadn't been as bad as this.

Before he got to the dip, Tomas let go and fell into a walk. The staff stopped him from stumbling and he had to stop from checking himself. There were many more people in this area, some in cloaks and hoods like himself, others in modern dress and yet more in foreign clothing from other countries. They popped in and out of the Corridor, no one glade taking any particular type of person.

The entrances to these glades had different markers to the usual white stones, Tomas was pleased he'd been told what to look for. He passed a stone carved with a many armed god, most of the people coming in and out of that one had a darker cast to their features than he did. He made a wild guess that it might be one of the Indian gods. Another he could have sworn was a medusa, the knots in its hair sporting both eyes and fangs.

He needed to know more and the only way was to investigate. Tomas stopped at a stone staff about six foot high and wreathed in ivy leaves. There were a mixture of people coming in and out of this entrance, he wouldn't stick out. He took a deep breath and stepped onto the track leading to the grove.

Chapter 16

Tomas stopped in awe, the track had led to a huge grove with massive oak trees surrounding it. The pool took up a large area with a grassy sward in front. Behind was the standing stone and a statue of a mature woman, her lips parted in a smile as she looked down into the pool. Unlike his own, this statue dominated the grove and towered over the temple behind it.

Tomas tried not to look at the statue and hoped being here wouldn't trigger any alarms. No one took any notice of him, those in the glade quietly talking, a good number of them were women. He wasn't sure what to do now that he was here, maybe he should look in the temple. With the path leading only one way, the standing stone loomed higher as he walked towards it. He couldn't help glancing into the pool as he passed it and noticed that the moon was just beginning to show. Tomas tried to walk faster and almost groaned at the feeling creeping across the glade.

"Hello little death worshipper." A voice purred into his ear and he turned, his heart thumping to see an older woman dressed in robes draped to show her figure, similar to the statue. He'd had many women of her age and size in his arms over the years, his hands instinctively knew the soft curves they'd find if allowed. It seemed polite to slide his hood back and bow a little, she was a god after all.

"How do I address you my lady?"

"I am Mother Nature."

"The Mother Nature?" Tomas almost winced, he was sounding like Stef.

"Just a Mother Nature." The god looked amused. "I don't generally accept those that have been taken but I might make an exception for you." She was eyeing Tomas up like a man would an attractive woman and he was finding it more than a little disconcerting.

"Thanks but I'm not staying." He tried to shift out of the way, not sure how much offence she would take.

She raised her voice a little, "Your god is another aspect of myself you know, nature and death are interconnected. Are you sure I can't persuade you to stay a little longer?" A scent weaved across him and he found himself relaxing, against his wishes.

"You know her?"

"No, I can just tell certain things, we all can." Her eyes had the twinkle of experience and he had to remind himself this was a god he was dealing with.

Tomas jumped as an arm was slipped around his waist and a hand touched his face. He hadn't noticed the woman coming close, all his attention had been on the god in front of him. This was bad but at least he'd learnt that the larger gods obviously didn't mind others coming onto their territory. He moved the woman out of the way and tried to ignore what his body was telling him. This younger body was useful but sometimes it gave problems, he knew better than to pay attention to it.

"Why not stay and help my worshippers for a short while. I'm sure it'll be an enjoyable experience and if I'm feeling generous then I might tell you what you need to know."

"I thought you were a god of nature my lady?"

She laughed, "What is more natural than sex and death?"

The woman murmured in his ear. "My lady's favours are intoxicating, let me help you enjoy them."

Tomas swallowed, his body was definitely reacting and she was barely touching him. The god's smile was in the distance as the woman's skin darkened to olive and her hair to black, gleaming dully in the half light. Perrette's brown eyes gazed into his, her breath was sweet and his hands instinctively drew her closer. The press of her hips against him, he could feel the same rise of lust they'd had all those years ago, the frantic coupling, the fabric of her skirts wadding under his hands. As he dipped his head to kiss her, his glance fell on a man sprawled against a tree, his expression was idiotic and his hand was in his trousers. Intoxicating - he remembered Chris' letter saying that the gods were emotional vampires. He pulled himself away from the woman and the illusion failed, her eyes were the wrong shade of brown and her skin and hair far lighter than Perrette's.

His voice was rough as he said, "Thanks, but I think the price may be too high."

The god laughed, completely unoffended, "It was worth trying." She waved a hand and the woman shrugged and left. "What are you looking for little death worshipper?"

Tomas took as deep breath, clearing his head. He didn't ask how she knew he was after something. "The god of mischief."

Her face darkened and then cleared, "He is very closely guarded. Be careful for your own god's sake."

"Can you tell me where?"

"You have told me my price is too high, if you would like to reconsider?"

"No, but thank you all the same." He bowed to her and walked away quickly, keeping his thoughts under strict control.

Tomas stopped just before walking onto the Corridor to compose himself and surreptitiously adjusted himself. Al-Kiron had been keeping quiet, he couldn't tell if she was upset with him, he had rather pushed her hand in bringing him here. He shrugged, his time with Stef had forced him into thinking slightly differently and that was never a bad thing. Too long thinking in the same way meant trouble, he'd been caught out many times by that. With any luck, those he was moving against wouldn't have that experience. He slotted into the heavy traffic on the Corridor feeling cheered that it appeared easy to slide into a god's territory without causing too many problems. He was going to have to find Chris' god and take a look at this map. He swore quietly, knowing that Chris would be expecting him to turn up at some point.

The route to the glade marked by a set of columns came too soon. As he went to step off the Corridor, a party of armed figures pushed their way through the people going in. There was a Degenerated in front on a leash, it dipped a hand down to knuckle sideways and moaned at the whip flicking over its shoulders. Tomas stepped aside with everyone else, thankful for the hood on his cloak. He ducked his head down, not wanting to be noticed.

He glanced up again just as the last of them went by and saw a familiar slender figure in her black jacket. Tomas felt an almost physical jolt at seeing Perrette so soon after having been a plaything for the god in the glade. Their eyes met and he went cold, not sure what she would do and doubting Stef's idea to rescue her god. Perrette's face tightened and she turned away calling over to another man with a laugh. He didn't relax until they'd stepped onto the Corridor and flashed into a blur.

"Any idea what that was for?" Tomas tried a friendly grin at the man next to him in relief and hoping for another garrulous bystander.

Not this time, the man glanced at him once and grunted, "Hunting that poor bastard who came through. They heard the noise as his god dragged him in for the first time and have been asking questions. Degenerated'll sniff them out." He shouldered his way onto the Corridor and disappeared into the crowd.

The noise? Tomas remembered the ringing in his ears as he'd lain by the way marker, he'd not had that either time before. Yes, he'd been stunned but that had been more by the transfer than anything else. Had it been deliberate or was it to do with forcing her hand? Those around him were moving again and he made himself pay attention to what was happening, he needed to stay alert here. He stepped back onto the Corridor, trying not to flinch at the shadows passing through him.

The columns were in front, towering over him and the other people walking down the track. The route itself was also lined with pillars, a formal separation between the trees and wilderness. The mist channelled itself between pillars and trees, streaming towards the glade in a way Tomas hadn't seen before. The odd cries and noises of the forest were drowned in the murmur of humanity. In the glade itself, the pool and stone were surrounded by what looked like a large village, closer to a small town. He wondered if the gods actually made these buildings or if people had brought them in, one block at a time. The statue was of a man, his forehead pinched in a frown as he gazed at a scroll, an abacus in his other hand.

Tomas edged past it with everyone else, bowing his head and walked swiftly down the path as though he knew where he was going. All the buildings were in the same Grecian style and of a blinding white stone although why they made him blink, he wasn't quite sure – the light was the same dusky half-light as it always had been.

There was a crowd of people coming and going next to the side of one of the biggest buildings. He shoved his way in to look and saw a man on a short ladder putting wooden tiles decorated with designs into slots. Some he moved around, others stayed while the crowd jostled each other, commenting on their positions.

Tomas noticed another man behind a table with a smaller crowd in front. Two larger men stood behind him, Tomas knew the look of bodyguards when he saw them. The man kept up a patter all the way as the other man put up the tiles. Slips and money were exchanged, people commenting, laughing and groaning. It had the strange air of a festival. Tomas blinked as he heard the language of betting odds and turned to look at the wall again.

There were rails under the tiles and smaller posts ran along them. The man on the ladder climbed down and used a pole to shift and lock the markers into place. There was a final flurry of slips and noise and Tomas heard the man's voice rise above and call for tomorrow's bets. He stepped towards the walls, staring at the tiles. There had to be at least fifty or maybe more and there was something very familiar about it. Every tile had a simple picture on it or sometimes a single word, not necessarily in English. The markers weren't spaced evenly either.

Markers – was this the simplified map that man had been talking about? Tomas followed the tiles, searching until he'd found one with a many armed god on it and smiled viciously, he'd been right.

"Can I help you sir?" The voice in his ear made him jump. Tomas wheeled around, his staff held at a diagonal to his body. The slim man held his hands up with a smile. "I wondered if you would like to make a bet? Some say it's a simple form of worship here."

"Who too?" Tomas didn't like the idea of helping a god who was after killing his own.

The man laughed, “It depends what you are betting. Come and take a look.”

The crowds had dispersed and the two heavies were in the process of fastening up an iron bound box. Tomas looked down on the table to see a smaller version of the map on the wall with numbers under each tile.

“So people are betting on where the gods move to next? That’s a bit profane isn’t it?”

“There are worse things to do and it provides entertainment.”

“And these are all the gods?”

“They are all the gods within a short radius of this glade. I would need a table the length of the Corridor to capture every god.”

The wording caught Tomas and he stared hard at the man. He didn’t resemble the god on the plinth, he was dressed casually in modern clothes and his voice held a faint London twang. He could have been a young forty year old or a twenty something who’d lived a hard life, Tomas couldn’t tell. The man didn’t blink as he was studied. Tomas transferred his gaze back to the tiles, “Why the pictures, why not names?”

“Because most know them by the symbols standing in front of their groves. Those that don’t have a symbol will have something that could be connected with them.”

“Do I make a bet on many moving or just one?”

“Some bet on others shifting a certain number of places or only the one. It’s your choice.”

No names, only symbols, how could he tell which was which? Tomas put his finger down on a tile, “Why doesn’t that one have any numbers underneath it?”

The man sighed, “Because I don’t allow sure bets.”

“Everyone knows where that god’s going to move?”

“Everyone knows that god will not be moving.” He held Tomas’ eyes with his own.

Tomas dropped his gaze to study the tiles, noting the positions. He stuck his hand in his pocket and found a coin. He held it out to the man, “I’d like to make a bet.”

“Of course sir.” The other man had a slip of paper and a pen ready to write. The two heavies had long since carried the box away and were waiting by the wall, just out of earshot.

Tomas dropped his voice, “I will bet that this tile will move by the end of the day.” He put a finger on the tile with no number under it.

“I cannot accept that sir.” The man had gone white.

“You said that it was a form of worship?” Tomas flipped the coin onto the table, “I’m not a gambling man but that god can have it if it’s a worship, he probably needs it.”

“Agreed.” The man held out the piece of paper as though in a dream and Tomas felt a strange buzz through his fingers as he took it.

“Don’t worry about me collecting my winnings, I’ll take my payment from the god himself.” Tomas picked up the tile, put it in his pocket and walked away.

Chapter 17

Tomas walked swiftly out, the tile clutched in his pocket. He now knew where Dar was, he just had to get out of here without… The scent of sanctity floated over him and he muffled a swear word – too late.

He composed his face and made a short bow as he turned. "My lord."

"Very few sneak in without me noticing, fewer still having laid a bet with my gambling man." The god held out a hand. "The tile please."

No one else was paying attention to them. Tomas passed over the tile, the dagger design flashed once before it disappeared. It didn't change any knowledge he had and yet it felt as though further chains were being snapped around Perrette. "You don't mind me being here?"

"Why should I? Little death worshipper, you are no threat to me." What had been a term of affection from the nature god was an insult from this one.

"May I ask your name my lord?"

"I am Money. I have been a god since trading began. People worship and desire me, kill for me." The god's pinched features glowed as he held out his hands in benediction to the grove.

"So you're not going to smite me down?"

"I will let my followers know you're here shortly, I like watching a good chase especially when so much is at stake. They want you badly I believe." The benediction turned into a savage smile and Tomas was sharply reminded of Chris' words.

"Why?"

"If your little god dies when you are here then you will turn into one of these." The god pointed into the pool and Tomas looked despite himself. A view of a dark hall underground, flames lighting the way and then a door opening. Tomas recoiled, not believing what he'd just seen. All the arms waving, the empty soulless eyes and bared teeth hit a naked spot in his psyche.

Panting, he stepped back, "That's not true."

"Well we shall see, shan't we?"

It was all a game to this god, the emotions running high and feeding him. Tomas suppressed his anger and the god laughed. "May I have your permission to leave?"

The god waved his hand, "I will give you a lead, not a large one but a lead never the less. Run priest of a minuscule god and my hounds will chase you."

Tomas didn't think - he ran and not just because he'd been told to. He wanted to get out of this sick glade. Money had never been important to him, only as a necessity to live. Working had always been a way to ground himself in everyday life and he'd discovered that too much money divorced him from that.

His mind was in turmoil, he had to protect his god. One way was to get out of the Hall and back into the real world but what about Stef? Had they already found Al-Kiron? Much as he had always hated their connection, she was vulnerable if they found him. They had been together too long, he couldn't just abandon her. Tomas panted harder, dodging those walking slower, he had to find Stef and Al-Kiron needed him. People were now jumping out of his way as he reached the Corridor. He stumbled to a halt, leaning on his staff and what about Dar?

He swore, that bastard god had known what he was doing, he was being pulled in three directions and he had so little time. Tomas swallowed. He didn't know where to find Stef, he could be anywhere. He had to give up the idea of finding him despite Al-Kiron telling him that she would cut his tie. Would she do that to him? Would he then become one of the Degenerated?

Tomas almost groaned out loud at the amount he didn't know. The grey skin and tattered clothes, how could he have not realised that they'd once been worshippers like himself? Al-Kiron had shown him Stef going grey but not like that, the reality was far worse. That woman he'd killed by the way marker, who had she been? The smile she'd given as she'd died, had death really been that welcome? He squeezed his eyes tight, he couldn't help Stef. He didn't have enough knowledge of this place to know how to help his own god. That left Dar.

Tomas lifted his chin, making himself recall the table with the tiles. The knife tile had sat further from the tile with the columns, and still further from the one with an ivy covered staff and the many armed god. He was making guesses here but they did match up to what he'd seen. He span around to face the correct way on the Corridor, breathing hard. Money's hounds would be after him, if they found him or Stef then he and his god were as good as dead. He had to free Dar so Perrette could give him the knowledge he needed. He felt his rage build and reached out to pull himself along the path, his surroundings blurring.

With every step he took, his anger grew. He had no shadowy wings coming over him this time, Al-Kiron kept herself small. He didn't need her, every injustice he'd lived in his long existence, every slight added to his rage. He'd been happy in his tiny life before his father had become ill, he'd not been allowed the pleasure of growing old or living normally. That first day of walking in a body not his, the terror of killing for the first time, easy… so easy… The struggle to balance himself so he could live in a normal society and knowing she could break that balance on a whim to make him do her will.

Tomas concentrated on the image from the tile, the dagger balancing on its point, waiting to fall in any direction, Perrette holding the knife by its blade to throw it. He no longer cared that freeing Dar would help her, for once he wanted to kill something purely for the pleasure of it. He pulled himself towards that image, feeling the weight of it in his mind.

A moss streaked white stone appeared in front of him, he slammed down his staff to stop himself from stumbling and it bent in the strange dynamics of the Corridor. There was no way of telling whose stone it was and yet he knew it was Dar's. Without stopping to look, he tore down the green pathway, noting in a subconscious part of his mind that it was over grown, the mist twisting past to grasp him with its white fingers. A clattering announced cribbet were around, he ignored them

He barely saw the glade as he ran in, the pool was surrounded by moaning Degenerated, they were corralled from getting close to the standing stone and statue. His mind wouldn't allow him to think of them as human. The first of the beasts took the full force of his hatred, it was slung across the glade with a single blow from his staff. The next leapt at him and he flung out a hand, the black streaking out without a thought. It died with a moan, its mouth gaping in a broken smile. The Degenerated launched themselves at him, not caring about their dead comrades.

Tomas welcomed them, sending them to his mistress, the years dripping through his fingers. He spent his anger on killing them, tearing through them as though they were tissue paper and all too soon the glade was quiet. He leant on his staff, his vision beginning to clear, knowing that very shortly he'd feel horrified by what he'd just done. A rattle of scales and he whirled to strike his staff against the leaping cribbet. The black flash sliced through it, the pustules bursting in a foul smelling pop. The rest of the cribbet rattled their scales in an impotent defiance and faded into the forest.

Tomas leant on his staff panting and stared at the pool, no moon was to be seen in its reflection. The statue of the slender man was still in one piece, he assumed that was a good sign. The face of the statue held a smile not unlike Perrette's, a touch of mischief in the curl of the lips.

"Well, I believe you owe me Dar."

"It would be far easier and cheaper to pay you the odds on the table."

The voice came from behind him as the moon slowly appeared in the pool at his feet and the scent curled around the glade. Tomas recognised the voice but his jaw still dropped at the sight of the bookie from the Money god's glade. "How?"

"I've been stuck there a while. It amused him to have me taking people's money for bets. He didn't think that I'd use it for myself."

"You used it?"

"I kept myself going by using tiny amounts over the years."

"And Perrette?"

"She's a fighter." The statement was said with satisfaction. "I chose well all that time ago."

He realised he was getting side-tracked. Time was ticking and his own god was in danger. "Dar, you owe me."

"You want a favour from the god of mischief? Not many would ask for such a thing."

Tomas made sure he phrased his words carefully, "I want Perrette to help me stop Al-Kiron from being taken the way you were."

"That's between you and Perrette, nothing to do with me. Thank you for helping me Tomas. I need to go now."

Tomas grabbed the god's wrist, "We had a bet Dar, I'm demanding payment." Dar's skin was slick under his as though made of a smooth marble.

"What makes you think you can compel me?"

There was a flicker of something in Dar's eyes under the anger, he couldn't tell what it was. Tomas bluffed and said softly, "It would be a huge sacrifice for my god wouldn't it? The life of another god?" He didn't know if he could do this, didn't know if it would work the same way. The only thing he did know was that these so called gods could be blocked and weakened by humans.

Dar was breathing heavily, his mouth tightening, "You dare to threaten me?"

"I dare to make you pay your debts or face the consequences. I don't know the extent of my abilities, shall we find out exactly what I can do?"

"You may have Perrette to help you, I cannot do anything else." Dar twisted his wrist out of his grip and was on the other side of the glade before Tomas could react.

"Hang on…"

Dar made an odd gesture and Tomas was silenced as he was flung out of the glade and into nothing.

Chapter 18

Tomas stumbled against the brickwork, grunting in surprise. Dar had flung him out of the Hall and back into the real world. He rolled around so his back was against the wall and swore quietly, he was in a city somewhere. It was night time, neon lights were shining at the entrance to the alleyway, the sound of cars and people talking as they walked past.

He unscrewed the staff quickly, wrapping it into a bundle with the cloak. The package tucked neatly under his arm. He swore again as he adjusted his belt, his shirt was also straining, although his jacket mostly hid the bulge. Tomas looked at his hands, darker brown frog spots were starting to cover them, he must be late fifties or early sixties – not good. A chill cut through him and he shivered. He could feel his thought processes showing the edges of inflexibility and fought against the restrictions. So many years lived and the body still moulded the mind. Tomas slapped his pockets and found his cigarettes, lighting one brought the warmth of normality back and he forced himself to think. He needed to find a place to stay, and before everything shut for the night.

A quick check of the rest of his pockets showed he had very little cash left and no way of telling what time it was. Tomas swore, it looked as though he was going to spend a cold night out unless he was lucky enough to find a homeless hostel somewhere. He also had to find Perrette.

Gloom descending, he walked out of the alley into the main street and blinked. Dar had put him back at the bar where he'd first seen Perrette. The walls of the bar had been filled, the doors were waiting to be repainted and a large sign declared that the bar was still open for business. The flowers for the dead were obviously not putting anyone off, people were still coming in and out. He had just enough cash for a whiskey or a meal elsewhere. Tomas looked at himself in the reflection of the window, he was a little dishevelled but just about reasonable. He shifted the belt under his slight paunch to make it more comfortable and decided to go for the whiskey.

The bar was noisy, the lights bright and people were enjoying themselves late after work. The smell of tapas hit him and his stomach rumbled. Just one drink, a chance to think about his problems in the warm and then out into the street again. He knew of places where he could sleep, it wouldn't be comfortable but he'd be safe and he'd found food before now in similar situations.

Tomas dumped the end of his cigarette in the saucer and started pulling all the change out of his pockets to count it as he signalled to the barman. He ignored the look he was given and winced at the price. He'd just finished pushing the coins into a pile when several notes were slapped on top.

"Make that a double please, I'll have a large red and the tapas for two from your menu."

Tomas barely had a chance to see the barman blink in surprise when a pair of arms enfolded him, pulling his head down for a kiss. His own hands slid around Perrette's waist as though they'd always meant to be there. Nothing else mattered, the noise of the bar fading through the sweet intensity. They parted and Tomas was left half stunned, his body still tingling from holding her. Perrette ignored him to pick up the glasses and walked away to a table in the corner.

"Whatever you've done to deserve that, can you let me know? I'd like one too." The quip came from a man propping up the bar next to him.

Even the barman smiled, “Your order will be ready shortly sir.”

“Excuse me, I need to follow my whiskey.” Tomas gestured towards Perrette, playing up to the comments with a wry smile and walked away.

He slid into the seat opposite, “What was that for?”

“Thank you for rescuing Dar.” She buried her face into the large glass, took a big gulp and then slapped him hard, open handed around the face. “And that’s for threatening him.”

That stung, he put up a hand to rub it and felt an irrational laughter building up. Perrette was in front of him, he’d actually survived threatening a god with death and she’d slapped him for it.

“It’s not fucking funny. He’s pissed as hell.” Her face was furious. Tomas couldn’t help it, he sniggered. He took a large swig of the whiskey and choked as it burnt. Water streamed from his eyes as he coughed, clearing his throat. “Serves you fucking right.”

“Did you do that?” He wiped his face.

“Might have.” She looked smug. “You deserved it. Would you really have killed him?” Her voice turned wistful.

“I don’t even know if I could.”

“Hang on, your god, she’s one of the old ones isn’t she? Didn’t she put any limits on what you could do?”

He lowered his voice, “She didn’t tell me anything when it happened. All I know is that if I don’t kill for her then I grow younger until I’m a child again.”

“She’s got you coming and going hasn’t she? Didn’t you think to bargain?”

“I had to, my father’s life...” His voice cracked. He shut his eyes, and composed himself, “I was a child when I became hers, I didn’t know any better.”

"Fuck," she breathed, "No wonder they're scared of you."

"What do you mean? Who?"

"She was desperate when she found you. She must have given you everything she had. They normally limit what you can do." At his look she said, "What that means is, the stronger she gets, the more you can do. You could bring down the entire Hall."

Tomas shifted, uncomfortable at this change in circumstance and the way Perrette was regarding him. He tried to change the subject, "They hunt down the gods with fewer worshippers and kill them off. Why?"

Perrette shook herself and took another gulp of wine, "You've noticed the mist and the fact that the ground's not too solid around the Corridor?"

"It's a little difficult not to."

"Well, belief makes everything stronger, more real. I've heard the theory that the mist is belief and when a god dies the mist around there streams out to a god of a similar type. The belief doesn't actually stop but it goes to a slightly different area."

"What happens if your god dies?"

"If you're unlucky enough to be in the Corridor when it happens then another god may take you on."

"Why unlucky?"

"Gods are jealous bastards, they don't like those who have sworn to serve others. They'll take you on but you have to take the consequences."

The hair rose on his neck, "Which are…"

"They let you keep living but only just. We call them Degenerated and they haunt the Hall until they die if not controlled."

"Shit." His bargain had been bad enough, made without knowledge of the consequences, this was worse, a living death. "Why do people accept it? Why…"

She cut him off, “How eager are you to die? Even after the amount of life you’ve had, could you just give it up?”

Tomas shook his head, he’d never been able to give up. His whole life had been an extension of cowardice. “So they kill the worshippers of other gods to make themselves stronger.”

“Mostly.”

He didn’t think he could become any more shocked, he would have expected a realm of gods to be a serene place, not this back biting extension of the human world. Under his stare, Perrette continued, “Sometimes they bring people through, find the echoes of a god who’s desperate.” She swallowed, “A god who’s dying, and let them take them. When they have stabilised then they cut the god off and kill them.”

“The people?”

“No, the god.” Her voice was soft. “The people then turn into Degenerated because they are desperate and will accept any god to stay alive.” She’d nearly finished the wine. A shadow above them made them both jump.

The waiter smiled, nervous at their expressions. “Your food.”

“Thank you.” Tomas wasn’t feeling like eating.

Perrette picked at a piece of bread, shredding it as the waiter left. She spoke in a rush, “They discovered how to herd the Degenerated several hundred years ago. That’s how Dar’s been trapped all this time, he did a lot of fast talking to convince them that having a god who can influence small things in their favour would be a good thing.”

“He gave you to them.”

“He stopped me from becoming one of them.” The blaze of anger burst from her sharply.

"And saved his own skin." Tomas wasn't convinced, he didn't trust that smile he'd seen on the god's face.

"Dar has survived many small deaths, I'm not sure how but he's told me he loses something every time. He'd rather not if he doesn't have to and he plays the long game, he wants to survive as well." Tomas snorted and started attacking one of the plates, he was hungry now he'd had the chance to warm up and the whiskey was beginning to dull the shock. Perrette shook herself and continued, "Still, the herding was infrequent until they discovered about bringing people across. They simply couldn't find enough small gods and their followers have to be in the Hall when the gods are killed so they started bringing innocents in. She took a deep breath, "People with no connection and letting them go in the Corridor. You've felt the attraction, even with a god, it's still there."

Tomas stopped eating, "That's sick."

Perrette nodded, "The gods love emotion and belief, they feed off it but even they are getting uneasy."

"And they've been using you."

She snorted, "Dar's the opposite of destiny, he spits at fate and so do I. I have my own small tricks to lever the way things can go. Occasionally they threaten me and get Dar to do a bigger trick."

"You're his last worshipper?" She nodded. "I've seen you so many times over the last few centuries, why?"

Her answer chilled him. "They want you. I've tried to put them off but they've been closing in on you for a while. Because you stayed small and they weren't sure about you, they were finally desperate enough to try any means to push you into the Hall. They have people who can follow your line back to Al-Kiron once they have you."

"Why have they been looking for that long when they weren't sure about me?"

"They know that Degenerated will follow a stronger Degenerated. I think originally, they wanted to turn you and use you like that or simply just to eliminate you because your god was perceived to be small. Now…" She paused and finished her wine. "They want to find out precisely how strong you are. They want to turn you and use you for threatening the gods themselves."

"Fuck."

"It's not just Chris who's after you, others have heard now and are interested. The one who kills Al-Kiron is likely to get you for their god. They'll win kudos for that, extra favours will be granted."

"And Chris has Stef." They'd follow his line back to their god, she'd be surrounded and he'd be brought to heel. Could he allow himself to die or be used as a weapon? The simple pleasures of making bowls, his hands covered in clay and the crack of his skin when it dried. He'd never wanted this.

Perrette jerked her head up, "No, Chris was still looking for Stef when Dar pulled me out after you'd freed him."

"What?" Tomas couldn't believe what he was hearing.

"Stef came into the Hall under his own steam. He brained one of Chris' followers in the toilet of that pub you were in and then dragged the other through. We found him by the way marker."

"Who, Stef?"

"No, Bill. Stef's a competent fighter under his amiable exterior, he's a black belt in Tae kwon do, among other things. Anyway, Stef's been leading everyone a merry dance through the Corridor. For someone who's only been there once, he's been doing really well."

Perrette laughed at his expression, “I knew Stef had been, he had a rip in his back right pocket. He normally keeps his phone there.”

Tomas said grudgingly, “You’ve a good pair of eyes.”

“It’s part of my job description.”

Her smugness rankled, “And how many times did you notice me over the years?”

“A fair number when you were between certain ages, I didn’t know you could change it.”

“Did you call the bailiffs that time in Ticha?”

She fiddled with her empty glass, suddenly finding it interesting. “I was told to distract you. I did.”

Tomas choked down the query as to whether she’d actually enjoyed their encounter, there were few other ways a woman in those times could have distracted a man. He wondered if she’d had to do others things as well to stay in favour and suppressed that thought as well. “It certainly worked,” he said lightly. He picked up several olives and ate them.

“How old or young can you go?”

“From the cradle to the grave. I looked for you, you know.”

“I noticed.” She flushed and dunked a scrap of bread in oil.

He smirked. “But not all the time. Have you got a plan for finding Stef?”

“Not more than Chris has, it’s just a case of following his trail. Chris has an advantage in that he has a Degenerated to help but you should be able to ask your own god for pointers.”

Al-Kiron, she’d been keeping herself quiet for some time, was she hiding herself the best she could? He was getting a nasty feeling about all this. “How much can I trust you?”

"You can't." She looked him straight in the eye. "I worship the god of mischief."

"At least you're being honest, or is that an oxymoron?"

She laughed, "I'll do what I can for you. I owe you one but if it comes to your skin or mine… I'll save myself."

"Fair enough. We're going back to the Hall." He scooped up his bundle.

Perrette glanced at the plate of half picked at food. "Now?"

"Yes, I've a bad feeling and paying attention to them has kept me out of the bailiff's reach on more than one occasion."

She sniggered and reached for his hand.

Chapter 19

Tomas walked them back to the alleyway. It was a similar time of night to the one where he'd been shot at, he turned his collar up as it began to rain, a sharp sweep of wet that took his breath away. "I'm not dressed for this."

He dumped the cloak in Perrette's arms as he assembled the staff, screwing the ends together tightly. The carvings still didn't quite match, he'd need to get a pair of mulgrips to tighten the screw further.

She stroked the cloak and then looked hard at the staff, "Hang on, where did you get all this?"

"Someone died," he said shortly.

"You killed them?"

He had to stop himself from twitching, he knew that tone. "No, a Degenerated did. I killed the Degenerated and picked this staff up with the cloak."

"Was it a small nervous chap, in his twenties?"

"Know him?"

"Yes," her voice was soft. "His name was Andy, he only got mixed up in this mess by accident. He wouldn't have harmed a fly."

Tomas paused, "I'm sorry, I wasn't thinking straight when I came through. If I'd have known I'd have done something." He was so used to being on his own, to assuming everyone was indifferent or hostile to him.

"There are clashes all the time between gods and their followers, my case shows what can happen but it never used to be this bad. People know now that you can bring others through and use them to kill the smaller gods who are just trying to survive. The belief has to go somewhere and the emotion that's generated..."

He finished screwing the staff together and hefted it, "So no one's safe anymore?"

"No and the uneasiness will filter back into the real world."

Tomas reached out to take his cloak and flipped it round himself. "I just want to keep my god alive."

"We all want to do that." She looked sad and then squared her shoulders, "Have you got a plan?"

"The start of one, have you got a weapon?"

"Have now." Perrette flipped a knife end over end and tucked it into the back of her trousers with a grin.

He snorted at her change of mood, "That won't do you much good."

"I can throw it."

A sudden absence made him reach for his own knife, "Hang on, that was mine."

"Just worshipping my god…" She laughed at his face, the mischief he'd seen in her god breaking through. He wondered if he showed any similarity to his own and shrugged it off.

He held an arm out, "Ready?" Perrette laughed again and slid her own arm around his waist, fitting as she always had done.

"Dar won't help with the transfer, he's too busy hiding."

"That's fine with me." Tomas closed his eyes, asking for what he wanted. She was as leary as he was about drawing attention to himself. She was hesitant and then the night air went black and he felt himself stream through the ether.

They stumbled, falling into the long damp grass. Tomas caught Perrette, cushioning her fall, the staff across both their bodies. Her hair fell around both their faces, curtaining them from the strange woods. He gazed into her eyes, too aware of her perfume and her body resting against his. She slid her arms around his neck, pulling herself up his body and closer, dipping her face to kiss him.

It was like being back in the woods all those years ago. The feeling of her lips, his hands against the unfamiliar material of her jeans. She was like him, no worries about watching her grow old or infirm. His body was responding to her and his arms tightened. This was what the nature god had promised and more, he snugged her into him, one leg sliding in between hers, his fingers intent on exploring further. That interesting gap where her shirt had become untucked beckoned and the staff rolled out of his grasp, slid and kept sliding.

"Fuck," Tomas broke the kiss and grasped for it as it nearly disappeared into a sward of grass. He grunted as their combined weight twisted his spine and pulled the staff back into the crock of his arm.

Perrette wasn't paying much attention, her face still inches away, "Hmm… This body's definitely got potential, you know there's something about an older man…"

"Stop mucking about. I don't change that much." Tomas rolled her off him, disturbed by how much she was distracting him in this older body.

She sniggered, unrepentant, "Ooo, not coping so we're getting all dominant are we?"

"I'm 'an older man' remember? I don't have the fucking energy for this."

"Balls, that's not what I felt." Perrette flicked her eyes down with a smirk and gasped. "Tomas…" Her legs were sliding down. She flailed, grabbing for him.

"Shit." Tomas pulled her back on top of him, feeling the ground becoming spongy underneath them both. "Right…" She twisted with him as he stood, sliding down his body to stand where he'd been lying. "Arms around my neck and hold on."

He could see her bristling at his tone and didn't care. Tomas poked at the ground, the end of the staff pushing through into nothing. The ground grew softer as he checked, could Al-Kiron help him from here? "What happens if we go through?"

"I don't know. They tried experiments a long time ago, we don't believe they survived."

He didn't need to know that, didn't want to think about people being shoved out here with no chance of escape. His stomach was clenching, one tussock appeared stable although it felt dodgy, there was nowhere else. He planted the staff and pulled Perrette into his other arm. It was going to be a long stretch, too far for her.

As he took that step, the ground sank under his other foot. They both clawed for the stable ground. The tussock gave way slightly as he stepped onto it, falling onto his knees and falling forwards. Perrette landed on her backside, her hands tightly locked around his neck. There was no back chat from her this time, Tomas could hear her panting in his ear and the flash of whites as she peered at their feet. He hauled them up again and began the slow testing, finding another hummock a little closer. The rattling of scales nearby made his blood run colder.

"Put me on your back, I'll hold them off." Perrette's voice was little more than a whisper.

He swivelled her round him and she jumped, her legs locking themselves around his waist and pulling herself up high on his back. He tucked his cloak up over her knees and tilted his weight forwards to keep them stable. One arm around his neck, she reached for her knife. "Keep going. I'll help in every way I can."

Tomas took another step, this time managing to stay upright. Was it luck or was Perrette somehow rigging the draw? A shadow raced towards them from the side, the stilt like legs finding every solid piece of ground. Tomas envied the cribbet's speed. Perrette jerked slightly as she threw, pulling him to one side and he slipped, jabbing the staff into unexpectedly solid ground.

The knife appeared in the cribbet's eye pit and it squealed, a metallic sound making his teeth ache. Perrette shook her hand, another knife appearing. She wriggled up his back again, tensing as it ran towards them. Tomas braced himself for the movement and stepped straight afterwards, swearing as it didn't stop running towards them. It was too close and her knives weren't stopping it, with one foot on each piece of solid ground he lashed out with the staff, knocking it off its feet.

It squealed again as it lost its footing, sinking into the illusion they were trying to escape from. Another knife sank into the gap in between its body and leg armour and it collapsed underneath it. Tomas and Perrette stood frozen as they watched it sinking and scrabbling to stay above ground. The noise cut off abruptly when its head disappeared.

"I feel sick," Perrette whispered.

"Not here." Tomas prodded the ground in front, finding more and more of it becoming solid as they moved forwards. The beast sliding under what looked like normal grass had disturbed him more than he liked, even something as disgusting as a cribbet didn't deserve that. The trees came closer and the normal path appeared. Tomas helped Perrette off his back and held her as she threw up. He leant against a black boled tree and pulled her close, wrapping his cloak around them both. She sobbed against his chest while he kept an eye out for other dangers. This woman was a mass of intriguing difference, ruthless when needed but crying over a beast like a cribbet dying.

Eventually she lifted her head, sniffing. “That was horrible.”

“True, but at least it’s proven there’s a use for my manly but sagging chest.” He provoked her deliberately.

“Don’t get all bloody funny at me.” She slapped his chest.

“I think I’ve a right too, you lost my knife for me.”

“Bastard.” He chuckled and hooked an arm around her waist. “What do you have planned?”

“Not much really. I can ask Al-Kiron where Stef is but I doubt she’ll tell me. Chris left us a letter on Stef’s USB stick saying they could find out where she was from the oscillations on the Corridor. Is that right?”

Perrette wrapped her arm around his waist to bring him closer. “He’s an arrogant bastard. He was bluffing to an extent, they can get an idea but nothing concrete, however if they find Stef then yes, they’ll follow the trail back.”

They walked along the path, they could have been taking a stroll in an unearthly park with the tattered mist and the grunts and clicks around them. Tomas tried to think through his older brain and could only come to one conclusion. Sooner or later they would find her and he wanted to be there when that happened. “I intend to make a lot of noise then, if you’ll help. I want them coming to me.”

“Why the fuck would you want that?”

“I want to fight on ground I know. Al-Kiron’s ground is my ground. I don’t want to die anywhere else other than in front of her knowing I’ve done my best.” Sooner or later they would find her. Age-wise he was in his sixties now, he knew how many deaths he could take and it wouldn’t be enough. He could feel his fear beating at him, screaming at him to run away. He didn’t have the time to wait to become younger, maybe she would take some years from him like she had before, maybe she wouldn't. Either way, both he and Stef would be dead by that point.

"You are fucking mad."

He snarled back, "Got a better idea?" Perrette dropped her arm from his waist and twisted away. He let her, watching as she shoved her hands in her pockets, her head down. He sighed, "Look, if you don't want to help…"

She huffed, her shoulders straightening. "I'll help you, I may be able to twist Dar's arm in helping out as well."

"He'll die if you do."

She laughed, a brittle sound. "Dar's an expert at surviving. He's managed to slide past that point by getting another worshipper right at the last moment before." She waved her hand sharply, "So many gamble, he'll just manifest into a slightly different version of himself. The weird thing is the two of us."

"What do you mean?"

"We've both lived so long and yet we're frightened of dying."

"Stef said something similar, he said everyone was frightened of dying."

"I often wondered what would have happened if Stef had been chosen instead of Chris."

"Did you know either of them before?"

"No." She shook her head. "I was passed onto Chris after he'd started getting noticed. I'm not just given to anyone." She sounded bitter, "I'm considered high value and I might escape if nobody keeps an eye on me."

"Poor little woman."

She snapped back, "Don't be a fucking arse."

Tomas twisted, “Stef would sympathise at this point.” He could see Stef, his head tilted, waiting for more information.

Perrette agreed, “Stef’s bright. He’s good at what he does.” They stopped in the trees to see the Corridor in front of them. She looked up and down the deserted cobbles. “We’re a long way down the Hall here, I don’t think I’ve ever been so far before.”

“Not even when you’ve been hunting smaller gods?”

She winced, “No, even the smaller gods cluster together if possible, you find they shift away from those who have died and despite what they say, I think they actually have less control over where they move than they’d like. You said you’d never been to the Hall before?” At his nod she said, “That makes sense, bringing you here takes a lot of energy when everything’s so thin and with no experience of the Hall she couldn’t risk losing you. She must have been surviving on scraps for centuries.”

“Stop it, you’re making me feel sorry for her.” He offered his arm again.

Perrette snorted and let him, his arm tightened around her waist. She squeezed his in return, “Which way?” “Let’s get this over with then.” She tugged him onto the path.

Tomas pointed and started them walking, “Will they know we’re here?”

“Chris will have people checking, there are those sensitive to this sort of thing. His god’s been experimenting with what he can grant here.” She sounded disgusted. “There are strange rules, sometimes the experiments don’t work quite as expected and they go mad. They can sense what the god wants them to but getting the information out is difficult. Thankfully they don't last long."

"What do you mean?"

"This place isn't exactly human friendly. People sort of fade when they've been here too long. They just give up and die, I can't explain it." She shuddered and looked around, "This place really is desolate."

"She's still a fair way down, she must have brought us through to the safest way marker she could."

"And even that one was shit. Let's move a bit faster, I don't care if it'll call more attention to us."

"I thought you didn't like that."

"Fuck it, I want this over with."

Tomas wrapped the skein of light around his wrist and pulled himself closer to his god. The landscape began to blur as they walked, Perrette was right this area was desolate. There were few of the white stones marking entrances to the glades and most were worn by time or in many cases rubble. The trees lining the Corridor were massive and gnarled and even the mist that normally swirled around looked insubstantial. The only solid thing in this world was the Corridor, the large cobbles impervious to time or distance.

He slowed a little before they got to her stone, still hesitant about showing where she was. "We're here."

Perrette stared. "Good grief, Tomas, look at this." She waved at a larger pile of stones to the side.

"What?" He didn't see much difference.

"This used to be an old nexus." At his look, she clarified, "A place where the larger gods used to congregate. That may be why she's not moved. She's chained here by the memories. No wonder no one's found you before."

"I suppose it's fitting, a death god surrounded by the dead." Larger humps showed further on, covered by small trees and grasses. There was no sign of any paths to the glades, they had all disappeared.

"I sometimes wonder…"

"What?"

"I have a vague theory that the Corridor is linear like time, the older gods shifting constantly along it or dying out. The current nexus is so far away, maybe in a millennia it might be the same as this one."

Tomas shuddered, "Can you imagine what older gods would be like? Al-Kiron is bad enough."

"I don't think much changes." At his glance she clarified, "Basic instincts, most of us want a mate, to be warm, fed and have the chance to procreate maybe. Then slightly more sophisticated wants appear as the first are satisfied." Tomas' thoughts took a nosedive, the option to take if you couldn't persuade, to kill if you couldn't take. That's where his god came in.

He stopped them in front of the white stone and Perrette hung back a little. When he looked at her, she laughed. "I always get a little nervous meeting a new god."

"I think we all should. Familiarity makes us blind. Come on."

He slid his arm out from around her waist and walked down the path.

Chapter 20

The statue and the pool, the standing stone to the side, nothing had changed. Tomas flung himself down on his knees. “My lady.”

The pool brightened as a half-moon crept into view, shimmering across the surface. He closed his eyes briefly as the sweet scent of sanctity spread throughout the grove.

“You wish me to show myself. To cast myself at the mercy of others.” She stayed in the shadow of the long stone.

“I’m not hiding anymore, I’m not running. They’ll find you eventually, I’m just bringing the fight here.”

She took a step out from the shadows, “Strong words my Tomas and you have brought another Favoured here.”

Tomas twisted to see Perrette still standing, her hands shoved deep in her pockets. She inclined her head, “My lady.”

“Little trickster. You are as much of a survivor as my own.”

“He’s right to fight. They’ll take him if they can and kill you to use him.”

“Fight, I remember…” Al-Kiron raised her head and her face changed, “I remember the sacrifices sent to me, the drums beating, the fear.”

“Men have always fought battles.”

“These were not men, these were commanded by women. I was a blood god, to be worshipped every full moon. I was feared and my followers names were spoken in hushed voices.”

Tomas could hear the distant thud of drums in the distance, the memory of adrenaline coursing through his veins. He knew the addictive pull of conflict where every second was a lifetime. "What happened?"

"They declined and I declined with them. I became a little god, sharing my space with others." She waved a hand, indicating the crumbled gods in the groves next to hers. "Unlike them I hoarded my energy and hid, knowing I would face a long starvation. I waited for the right person and found them."

"I was a child." The old wound bled.

"You were a bright flame in a room of guttering candles. I chose well."

"What happened to my parents, my sisters? I came back years later and couldn't even find the town."

Al-Kiron sighed, "Your parents lived a further five years. Your sisters married and moved away. All happened as I promised."

"My father must have been in his thirties…"

"Your father was old. I had killed the little cells that had refused to die inside him and I kept killing them while he lived. Your parents died together in bed."

He was used to her sliding away. He was in front of her now, people were coming to kill her and he needed to know what had happened. "How?"

"The hillside was unstable a way up the valley. The land slipped one night and the water that had built up behind it poured out. They and the rest of the town died instantly. They never knew what had happened."

Tomas nodded and walked away to sit against a tree. Her words had been blunt and cool - individual lives meant nothing to her. He stared at the pool, aware of the warmth of Perrette as she sat down next to him and leant, for once saying nothing. He was conscious of Al-Kiron pacing the grove, touching the standing stone and watching the woods.

He felt nothing, just a relief that he finally knew what had happened to them. He could barely remember their faces, the echo of his sisters' laughter fading into the years but was it even theirs? The clamour of centuries rose up, men shouting, women crying, the hubbub of people living and dying threatened to drown him. Tomas pulled his knees up, burying his head in them and covered his ears unable to shut it out.

Perrette pulled them away, "Don't let it defeat you." She drew him close and held him while he stared into nothing, remembering the stream of events, hard seconds implanted in his memory. Faces and landscapes blurred into an intense flickering of a sharp's card trick.

He dragged himself out of Perrette's embrace, breathing heavily, "What about Stef, can you tell me where he is?" Al-Kiron didn't answer. He used the staff to pull himself upright, "Where is Stef?"

"They have him, I will cut him off."

"You will do no such fucking thing." Tomas ignored Perrette's noise of horror at him speaking to his god in such a way. "You cut him off and I will put signposts all the way down here, no, I'll lead them here myself and bare my throat for them to have me."

"He is not important."

"Fuck that. He's important to me." He slashed the air with his hand.

"You would not give yourself up, you know what you would become."

"I would be alone again if Stef died. I'm not having that. You will keep hold of Stef or you will have neither of us."

"You will not protect me?"

"Not if it means Stef's life."

She dropped her head, "They have him. They will follow his line here using the Degenerated."

"But they won't kill him, not yet." Perrette came to stand next to Tomas. "They'll keep him alive and in one piece just in case."

"Well?" He could feel his stubbornness grating against her, his refusal to give in, the same as he had survived year after year. Stef meant something to him, he'd been alone all this time. Even Perrette's presence wasn't the same, she was connected to another god.

Al-Kiron raised her head and close her eyes as though listening for a sound in the distance and said, "If I keep hold of him then you will protect me my Tomas?"

Relief filled him, "My lady." He knelt and felt her fingers in his hair.

"You must make yourselves ready, there is a band of Degenerated coming down the Corridor. I have never felt such a gathering, the Hall bends to their howling."

Tomas stood and looked around, there was nowhere he could stand and have them come at him one at a time.

"The woods will be unsafe here, they can only come along the path. Cribbet are likely to arrive when the battle starts, they like carrion and don't care what it used to be or if it's still alive when they start feeding."

He nodded at Perrette's words, half turning as the feeling faded from the grove and the moon disappeared from the pool. Al-Kiron had walked into the shadow of the stone and the line connecting them turned insubstantial – she was hiding herself.

"Trust in me, my Tomas." The words were a whisper in his ear.

"You've seen this happen before?"

Perrette looked white. "Yes, they'll try to surround her. Degenerated hate the gods, maybe it's because they used to worship them. Their presence blanks off an area so the god can't get through to the real world. Eventually the god dies."

"Does it take long?" Perrette shook her head. "So I need to stay close to her. If she dies then what will happen to Stef?"

"They will hold him close to the grove and make him available to the closest god. He won't have long."

"Another reason to fight hard then." He felt in his pocket and flipped something to her, "Catch." At her puzzled look he said, "Seen anyone survive this?"

"No."

"Then I bet you I will. Consider that coin a bit of extra worship, payment for any help your god will give." He flashed her a smile, no longer caring. He recognised this feeling, it bubbled up every time he'd been at war in the reckless knowledge that everyone apart from him would die. "Stand and cover my back."

Perrette shook her head, "Stand over here." She indicated the standing stone. "For some reason they go for this rather than the statue. Chris had the idea that it was some sort of ariel."

Tomas grunted in amusement, "A cosmic receiver, collecting prayers from the worthy."

She tilted her head, her face twisting in mischief as she began to say something and then jerked to attention. Tomas felt it as well, a shift in perception outside the grove. "They're coming." She looked sick, "I've seen this happen too often..." Her voice trailed off.

Tomas backed up closer to the stone, he could feel Al-Kiron sliding away and deliberately wrapped the thread of light around himself, anchoring himself to her. He wouldn't be able to stop the Degenerated from surrounding them, the grove was too wide. Tomas began to breathe deeply, "They've not dealt with anyone like me before, let's give them something to remember."

"You are fucking mad."

He grinned at her, "I'm terrified." His fear no longer mattered, every breath he took was a validation of living. The shift of his clothes against his skin, the feel of the mist, was this the real reason he'd sought out war zones? Because it made him appreciate what he had? Or was it him daring her to let him die? He shook his head, it no longer mattered. What was real and now, the moaning could be heard from the track. He tightened his grip on the staff in anticipation.

They burst out of the path and into the grove, spreading out in a slavering mass. Even this many humans would be difficult, these were different, they were fast and with claws at the ends of their fingers. Knowing that they'd been human didn't help, or that they'd once worshipped a god like himself. They were pushed forwards by those coming in from the back and a desperation to kill. Tomas readied his staff, knowing he couldn't get all of them, a murderous rage building - they wanted to kill his god.

Perrette was leaning against his back, her quick breaths a counterpoint to the thudding of his heart. "I've never seen so many, Chris must be desperate." A scream from the path, unlike the others, made the mass in front of them lurch forwards into a run. "My god…"

"What?"

"They've brought the Baron. I thought Chris said he'd never use him…"

"Bad?"

"He must want you very badly."

There was no time to speak further, the Degenerated were upon them. Tomas used both ends of his staff, jabbing and swinging high and low to knock them off their feet, he couldn't use the full length of it, there wasn't the room. The Degenerated had no tactics, no strategy, they just came in a huge swell of claws and teeth, swiping left and right. Perrette was throwing knives, her hands a blur. Every throw hit something vital, Dar had been forced into this battle as well. Even if he could sidestep fate and not die, her death would be an inconvenience. What about Al-Kiron? She was quiet inside him, waiting for something. He bellowed his rage, the Degenerated moaned and the scream from the back urged them on further.

A hand touch would kill them, the odd smile appearing before they were trampled on by their comrades. He grew desperate as they were forced back, the bodies piling up. One misstep and they'd be on him. The black light flickered out into the mass and killed several, more took their place. A rattling and the cribbet arrived, humped bodies and stilt-like legs adding to the confusion. They didn't care who they killed, anything dead was a feast to them. Tomas could hear the chittering above the moans as the battle became chaos. He couldn't use the staff and touch at the same time, this was a useless weapon in these circumstances. A rip as a set of claws went through his shirt, he was growing older at an astounding rate, he'd slow down soon and be unable to fight. Desperation pushed him, the line to his god was still insubstantial despite the energy going to her. He needed her to take more, to help him with this.

An odd numbing to one side, the Degenerated were coming too close to the stone. Perrette screamed, "I can't hold them off."

He couldn't let her down, all these years he'd worshipped her, resented her. They were starving her of her connection to his world, to him. The mass of faces, ripped flesh, the moans. Tomas let go of the barrier he hadn't known was there. His parents had died together, in their sleep. They'd had the chance to see their daughters married and had more years than they'd expected or even hoped for. The knot inside loosened, and he let it go.

He needed to use both weapons and hands, he gripped the staff and swept it to one side, a black arc appearing from the end and cutting the Degenerated off at the knees. Their deaths channelled through the connection and he felt her rise above him, her wings unfolding. The world turned red and black, visions of ages past, warriors flickered behind his eyes making those lesser beings tremble as they cried her name for mercy. Drums filled his ears, an unyielding incessant death beat designed to intimidate and fill opponents with fear.

Tomas bellowed his vengeance, the pounding of his heart becoming that of the drums, black flashes scything, the arcs whirling towards his enemies on a wind of death before they got to him. He could feel the pouring of life through him into her, his worship. He was nothing but her puppet in this and both Degenerated and cribbet died alike.

A wild elation filled him, no one could withstand them together. He would conquer the world in her name, she would rise again. He climbed the mountain of bodies, others scrambling to throw themselves at him and falling before his scythe. Stef no longer mattered, those holding him would die or Stef himself would. She would have millions of worshippers, her name rising in glory to the beat of the drums. Even Perrette paled into insignificance, she would beg to be his, promising him anything…

A scream pierced his revere and he swung to face the creature Perrette had called the Baron. It carried its own whip for driving on its inferiors. Unlike the others, this one was wearing a crude leather armour, a large obsidian mirror inserted into the chest plate. It strode with intent, the rips in its clothing showing stringy muscle.

Part of him was aware that there were few opponents left in the glade and those few were sliding away without anything to drive them. The cribbet also faded away, looking for an easier target. Tomas jumped off the pile of bodies, his mind filled with visions of death and glory. This puny creature would fall to his god, the same as the others. A woman was screaming something in the distance, his mind refused to pay attention as he walked towards his opponent.

The Baron lashed out with the whip, he twisted to avoid it and the dull light flashed off the mirror. His gaze was caught in its reflection as he saw an old man standing there, clutching a staff. His hands began to shake, he'd never seen anyone so old. The flesh was hanging off his face, pale and pasty. The air deadened around him, closing him off from the battle fever. The black blade flickered and went out, unnoticed. He grasped the staff, determined not to become distracted and failed, how could he possibly see or even move? Film clouded his eyes, making the figure walking towards him shadowy. The staff grew heavier and he needed it for support not fighting. The scream the Baron made became shrouded in cotton wool, his limbs became like lead. It was taking all he had to stand upright.

Something dragged at his arm making him stagger. He clutched at Perrette, she was shouting something about the Baron. He couldn't understand, his brain was functioning but not on the same wavelength. A crotchety irritation filled him at the silly girl. They were going to die, he couldn't harm a fly in this state. All those bodies piled around them and he was going to fail at the last hurdle. The most he could do was face his death in a fitting manner, he'd seen so many do this before, old men squaring their shoulders and finding a last courage to do what was right. Those who had no other place to go, suddenly being at peace with themselves, a decision made.

Perrette turned, her hair a whirl and flung a knife at the advancing figure. Her shadow tensed again, another knife in her hand, ready to throw. He felt rather than saw the whip flick again and she lurched back, clutching at her face, blood seeping out between her fingers. The red stood out in his blurred vision. Perrette had been in his life for centuries, the smiles she'd given him in so many different guises, the memory brightening his day to keep him going. A lifetime's worth of blood and death, the trust he'd discovered in his god, the final sacrifice, it all made sense.

"My lady, I am yours."

His voice came out cracked and was obscured by the rush of the channel opening up further between them. Energy ran down his limbs, breaking the spell of the mirror. It became a black lacquer again with no special powers to contain him. The Baron screamed and lashed out with his whip, Tomas twisted out of the way and the end of his staff flickered into life. The scythe cut through the whip like a knife through butter.

The Baron flung itself at him, moving fast to shift out of the way of the scythe and swiping with its claws. He drove it back, parrying its darting figure, unable to hit it with staff or blade. Nothing mattered apart from trying to kill this thing, he'd never seen anything fight the way it did and part of him was appalled at what his own body was managing to do, ancient as he must be. He couldn't stop, couldn't give up, his body fuelled by his god. The monster was equally driven, it wanted her death and nothing else would satisfy it. Both bellowed their rage at the unfair cards life had dealt them, neither able help what the other was. Tomas counted every second as a lifetime, hyper aware of every movement his adversary made. Spit flying out of the corner of its mouth, the slide of his own clothes across his arms and back, every detail noted. He couldn't keep this up forever, at some point there would be a fatal mistake made by one of them.

A dying cribbet lashed out a barbed leg, slashing the Baron's calf and it faltered for the briefest second before recovering to lurch out of the way of Tomas' strike. Off balance, it stumbled to the side and all of a sudden the battle turned. Tomas was now chasing it, forcing it to defend itself as it was unable to recover its former attack. He could feel Al-Kiron rising as it twisted to avoid him. He was going to slay this beast and send it to his god, victory would be his. The deep battle drums began, making his muscles surge in time, his sweeping weapon reaping the harvest owed to him.

The Baron stumbled to fall again, Tomas bellowed his triumph as it hit the ground and rolled sideways to avoid his blade. Too late he realised where it had manoeuvred him and Al-Kiron's anthem faltered in his ears. It sprang to its feet, no longer caring that it was leaving its back open to his attack and ran for the stone. For an instant he gaped and then charged after it, exhaustion replacing the adrenalin and making him stumble. Only Perrette stood between it and his god, determinedly flinging her daggers until she realised her own danger and turned to run herself.

Tomas could feel the numbness of the Degenerated Baron cutting his god off from him - he wasn't going to make it. He was two seconds behind, a lifetime of being unable to catch up and Perrette would die, Al-Kiron would die. The drumbeat stopped and in the deep silence, he flung the scythe in desperation.

It went, end over end in a black whirl, the blade flickering out and it struck the Baron in the back, knocking it to the ground. Perrette shrieked and stumbled backwards at the grasping claws. It wasn't enough, he could feel the keen from Al-Kiron and the glade trembled, it was too close to her. None of them would survive this, including himself. He flung himself full length into the grass, his hand reaching out and grasped its boot. The link he had was so thin and he let the Baron have everything he had. The scream it let out rattled the glade, deafening him. He barely heard the whisper that followed – "Thank you."

All was quiet. Bodies were piled high in the once beautiful glade, it was filled with the stench of blood, opened bowels and the broken pustules of cribbet. Perrette was sobbing somewhere, he needed to hold her, to let her know that they'd both be alright. He couldn't move, he was too old. He knew this feeling, it would all be over shortly, that final step and he would be free of his promise. The moon coming into the pool brightened the glade as did the feeling. The bodies no longer mattered, they were her due, no more.

"My Tomas."

He couldn't even move to acknowledge his god, his hands clutching at the ground impotently. Her pride in him meant nothing against the ragged exhaustion claiming him and he fell into the black pool of unconsciousness.

Chapter 21

Tomas slowly became aware that his eyes were open, his clouded vision struggling to focus through the mist. He couldn't move his arms and legs, heavy weights pulling them down. Soft touches came to his face and hair, he started to panic until he realised his head was being cradled on someone's lap, their arms holding him up against their chest. He groaned and didn't recognise the weak sound.

A voice shushed him, "You only just survived, she needs you to keep living."

He recognised the state he was in and he was amazed he wasn't older, more decrepit. His rage felt a distant memory under the cotton wool of age. The arc of the scythe as it took down the Baron, had his staff really changed like that? Something warm and wet fell on his face, he blinked and peered up in confusion. Perrette's face was a blur, her features looked youthful and delicate in the gaze of decrepit helplessness. He concentrated and made out her words through his muffled ears.

"He wants me to kill you, he says you're dangerous in a way I can't comprehend. I can't, besides the minute you realise you'll take my life as well."

The voice forced from his throat croaked as he spoke, "I couldn't, I'd die as well."

"Touché." Perrette forced a laugh. Her fingers caressed his hair and shoulders with a fierce possessiveness. It was exhausting being wanted in this way. He wished he were younger so he could take advantage of her mood. A shift in his mind and he closed his eyes, wondering how long it would take his god to allow him the dignity of dying.

A palsy shook his hand and he clenched it absently, his grip strengthening. The touching stopped, the body cradling him withdrew a little. He muttered to himself, wishing for a little sunlight through the leaves, a little warmth in the air. Something began to drain away and he braced himself for what came next despite not knowing what to expect. Instead the palsy stopped, his grip becoming stronger.

Tomas opened his eyes and raised his hand to stare at it. His vision had cleared, enabling him to see that the blue veins of age were hidden by healthy olive skin, the wrinkles smoothing. The frog spots shrank and faded, muscle filling out the torn shirt he wore. He glanced up, Perrette's face was loosely framed by her hair and he smiled, a dalliance in the woods wouldn't be bad but he doubted she'd let him.

She smacked his chest, "Stop admiring yourself. You wouldn't believe how creepy it is when that happens." Perrette touched his chin as though she couldn't stop herself, "She's taken years away from you, I'd say you're about forty. A nice bit of silver around the ears, nothing too obvious." She chuckled and bent to kiss him. Tomas let her, cursing inside that everything hurt – Al-Kiron hadn't taken any of that away.

He swung a hand up and caressed her face, allowing it to fall down to the neck of her shirt and untucked a single button, gravity drawing his fingers down to the next. He held her eyes while he did, caressing the cleft between her breasts. She let him undo another and caught his hand.

"One set of tits just like any other?"

"Oh I don't know, there are always surprises. You never know until you see. Unfortunately I'm in no fit state to take advantage of them." He winced as she shifted and swallowed when her slender hand slid under his belt buckle without undoing it. “That really isn’t fair.”

“Well, see one dick, seen them all.” Her fingers had certainly found the one part of him that didn’t hurt quite as much moving as he thought it might. “Although this one…” She trailed off smirking at his reaction.

“I’m at your mercy lady.” His voice had roughened. “Although maybe I’d die a very happy man if you’d put something else around there instead.”

“Cheeky bastard, I don’t think you need to worry about dying yet.” She kissed him again, harder this time and twisted to slide him onto the ground, not allowing her hand to stray. Tomas forgot his aches and pains as she pulled at his clothing, stripping him efficiently. Her passion caught him by surprise and ignited his own. Nothing mattered, not the glade full of dead bodies or the ever potential danger of cribbet or even the possibility of other people around. Her insistence in moving his hands to please herself, the smell of her perfume and her desperation for a release. They made love on the hard ground in front of his god, her on top and fitting as perfectly as she had before.

Tomas stared into the mist above them afterwards, his arms cradling her and felt a deep satisfaction running through him. He’d killed his enemies, straightened out his relationship with his god and had the beautiful woman he’d wanted for years make love to him. He smiled, life couldn’t get much better.

Perrette had relaxed onto his chest, her hair tickling him and gave the wicked little chuckle that had caught him so many years before, “For some reason I always get horny after a fight like this.”

That made him blink, had she done this before? He squashed the jealousy down, not wanting to spoil the moment. “Blood thirsty,” he kept the tone light. “Am I to be feeling used?”

“Consider yourself well and truly only wanted for your body.” She brushed her fingers possessively along his collar bone, her actions contrasting with her words.

Tomas relaxed again and ran his hands idly down her back, sweeping them round to cover her backside and enjoying the feel of her skin against his. “Do you remember when we first met?”

She wriggled her head deeper into his shoulder, “Yes. It was about twenty years or so after Dar had found me. It was unbelievably hard to function without a man around to vouch for me. I’d teamed up with another of his worshippers for the short term to get used to living outside of society. Everything depended on who you knew at that time, despite the paperwork side of things it’s actually easier to live these days.”

“That’s funny, I never used to have a problem.”

“You’re a man, it makes a difference. Anyway as you know, he got far too friendly with me and wouldn’t take no for an answer.”

Tomas remembered, he been working as a hired hand in the autumn. Moving around various small holdings in the area, harvesting and helping with repairs. Perrette had caught his eye as she had many others, slender and with the spark of mischief that made a man want to catch her and find out where it might lead to. Obviously the man she was living with had felt the same. He’d heard the neighbours discussing the spirited arguments before he’d met her and once he had, he couldn’t get her out of his mind.

He’d offered to do a number of days’ work on their small holding at a lower price just to get closer. He never expected anything else, he was several centuries old by that point and deliberately kept any dalliances or friendships brief. His decision had been swept away the minute he'd seen her walk into the barn with a cloth over her face. She'd not expected anyone to be there and had frozen. He'd helped her bathe the black eye and her companion had found them and had decided the worst. Instead of calling the bailiffs to arrest Tomas, he'd attacked him instead.

"You killed him. I didn't know what you'd done at the time."

He hadn't known that this man was like himself, there'd been nothing in his death to suggest anything unusual. They'd laid him out on his bed at Perrette's insistence and she'd gone to her neighbours while he went out into their fields to work as though nothing had happened.

"And you didn't stay afterwards." He'd watched the funeral, noticing her dry eyes during the traditions to send off the dead. No one had suspected him. He'd done his work and moved away, hearing afterwards that she'd gone to visit relations.

"The people in that place were suspicious of me and I decided I hated the country. I'm a city person, give me lots of people any time over nice views. I shacked up with a travelling entertainer for a while. I'd learned my lesson and taught him to respect my knives." She hesitated, "Your killing Estiene set off a chain of events and I ended up being Dar's only worshipper. I was caught about fifteen years afterwards by Garalt, a very clever man. He decided to hold onto me instead of killing Dar off completely when he realised I had uses."

"I'd apologise but he was an arsehole."

Perrette nodded and rolled off him to start doing up her shirt. "True, he never looked beyond his own time and expectations."

“I kept thinking I’d met someone like you over the centuries.” He watched her getting dressed, enjoying the view, not worrying about his own nakedness. “I didn’t know you were like me.”

“Garalt had me looking for other favoured, once he realised I had long life then I was passed along the chain of command as they grew old.”

“Why didn’t you betray me?”

“I was never entirely sure what had happened that morning and you never gave anything away apart from turning up occasionally.” Her lips tightened, “Because nothing could be pinned on you, I decided you were my ace and I never give an ace away willingly.”

“Is that all I was to you?” All those years and the wistful name he’d given her, had he been anything else?

“I’d look out for you and you never tried to hold onto me, that was enough.” She tilted her head at him, “Are you getting dressed?”

Tomas rolled over onto his feet and pulled on his clothes, wincing at his bruises. Never trying to hold onto her… he kept his tone light despite the sharp pang, “You know, we really must think about getting together more than once or thrice a century.”

“Maybe. She’s not lost much time has she?”

“What?” He turned while doing up his trousers. The bodies had disappeared while they’d been making love and a small stone building, reminiscent of a towerless chapel stood behind the statue. “That’s new.” He wrapped an arm around her waist absently as they walked up to it. Perrette was looking troubled. “What’s up?”

“They don’t build unless they’re intending to grow. It’s proving she has a surplus and can afford to waste it on things like this.”

"Well she did take all those deaths Chris kindly sent her way." He stopped and swore, remembering, "Speaking of Chris, where's Stef?"

"If Chris wasn't here then he'll be waiting for news to come back. He'll have Stef somewhere safe."

"Like?"

"In the Degenerated pit." She twisted away from him, "They tie them up and dangle them from the ceiling. It's not pleasant."

Tomas picked up his staff and hefted it having finished dressing, "Right. Looks like that's my next stop."

"I'm coming with you."

"You don't need to, it's not going to be nice." He intended it not to be nice, Chris had pissed him off one too many times.

"I've got my own bone to pick with Chris now I'm free, several actually." She flipped a knife meaningfully.

"Let's go then, I don't want to give him a chance to send any one else here."

At the entrance to the grove was a simple covered gate with a bench incorporated into it. Tomas chuckled, she was proving to have a sense of humour, he'd never expected a lych gate as her entrance. He stopped at the sight of the slender figure leaning against a post, cleaning out his nails.

Tomas said shortly, "Dar."

"So, you have been paid back in full." Dar smirked, "And with extras… I must admit, I quite enjoyed that while it lasted."

Perrette flushed and Tomas narrowed his eyes. "What is it you want?"

"My worshipper. Perrette, kill him now please."

She gaped and then snapped back, "Kill him yourself."

"He's dangerous. Perrette, kill him."

"Too bloody right I am..." Tomas took a step forward.

Dar raised his hands, "Don't threaten me worshipper of death."

"So I'm not a 'little death worshipper' anymore? Why?"

"You are a human. A pitiful creature with no ambition."

Something rang false. "I've lived centuries longer than any human. Why don't you kill me yourself?" Perrette's gasp made him take another step and Dar sidled out of the way. Tomas lashed out a hand and grasped Dar by the label of his coat. "You're frightened of me."

Dar laughed once, his eyes sparkling and Tomas was left with his hand holding nothing but thin air.

Chapter 22

"Fucking arsehole." Tomas was left staring at his hand. "So, you're going to kill me?"

"No." Perrette's reply was quiet.

"He could cut you off."

"The worst he'll do is make things difficult. I can help you by staying close and keeping an eye out for unexpected things. He's given too much to kill me off hand, they don't like to give so much out now and he's not taken anyone else on, he's not been able to since he was caught."

Tomas could feel his rage building at the emotional vampires playing this game with them. They weren't gods, maybe more powerful in some ways but not gods. Humans weren't pawns to be pushed around so they could continue to feed off them. He glared up and down the Corridor, hating the beings hidden in their groves.

As though in answer, the soft whisper came through his consciousness – "Do you hate me as well my Tomas?"

"Love and hate can be very close together my lady."

"Sorry?"

Tomas blinked at Perrette's query, not realising that he'd spoken out loud and shook his head, "I'm finding Chris, come if you want."

He strode along the Corridor, his anger burning brightly. He could feel the touches of the dead or dying gods in the glades plucking at him and he brushed them off as an irritation. The landscape began to blur as he pulled himself along faster and faster, his feet barely touching the ground. Perrette tucked an arm around his waist to stay in time with him. There was an odd shift in the Corridor in front of them, as though it was slowing them down.

She tugged at his arm, "There's more Degenerates ahead, can you feel them?"

"Good," he grunted. At her look he said, "That means Chris is still trying to kill us. It means he has Stef alive and they're in one place."

He'd wondered if they could slide through them like they did with people and discovered the Corridor slowed them down as they approached. It looked like another army, it filled the entire path with them keeping to the straight edges. The Corridor itself was deserted, no one stood along the sides to let them go by.

"Stay out the way."

Perrette opened her mouth to make a cutting remark and closed it again, she stepped behind him, her knife ready. Tomas held his staff across his body, his anger igniting the black blade and strode towards them.

The first shambled up to him in its odd movements, ignoring the fact that he was standing in its way. It folded with a sigh and he saw the whips stop and a scrambling of feet above the moans. Tomas cut through the Degenerated like butter, not caring that people were getting away, he'd get them later. His anger flowed in waves as he sent their lives as his worship, the channel between him and his god completely open. He felt her grow fat and replete and yet she took everything he gave without aging him.

"They're escaping." Perrette pointed out the Degenerated who'd split off from the back with no one to keep them moving in the right direction. Tomas mowed them down from behind, considering it a mercy mission of those unable to choose a clean death.

He stood panting after the last had been despatched, listening to the chitterings in the mist. The cribbet weren't stupid under their bony carapaces, they'd not attack him at the moment. "We'll catch them later."

"Who?"

"The drivers, they know what they're doing."

Tomas began walking again with a purpose. He ignored Perrette's worried silence behind him, knowing she was thinking about Dar's sly words. It made his temper glow hotter, all he wanted to do was to rescue Stef and live quietly. He could feel that dip in the landscape in what felt like miles ahead. Tomas bent his head and surged on, the dip slowly becoming more noticeable.

Perrette stumbled as they came to a halt close to the dip. Tomas caught her, "What's up?"

"I'm getting tired and we were a long way down. I'm really not surprised we didn't find her now."

"You can stay here if you want."

"No, I'm tired because I've been here too long." At his look she said, "Humans can't stay here for long, it's not actually a viable environment for us. I'll need to leave soon. I'm surprised you don't feel it."

"I don't feel anything."

"That's worrying." She put a hand to his forehead in an oddly maternal gesture. "If Al-Kiron's sustaining you to get through this then you're going to know all about it when you leave. Otherwise you'll end up falling asleep here and not waking up if you're not careful."

Tomas shrugged, "I'll leave after I've dealt with Chris."

She looked like she was going to protest and then shrugged, "You get this wrong and you'll both lose, possibly your lives. Be careful."

He ignored her warning and they walked at a more normal pace past the entrances. There were less people milling around the Corridor here. Tomas noticed people giving them startled looks and pulling back, some disappearing down the black stoned tracks to marker stones. He presumed their gods were giving them warnings to stay away. Then he glanced down and chuckled, he was coated in blood, the cloak with its hood across his face and the staff giving him a forbidding look. Perrette was somehow less covered although she walked with a swagger that invited anyone to do their worst with her.

"Do you think they realise we're trouble?"

She snorted and waved at the columns that flickered in the distance, "I hope you've got a plan."

"Yes, I'm making it up as I go along." His levity failed again as he contemplated going up against a man he didn't know. The swirling of the mist between the columns and the forest had an ominous feeling this time. "Do you know where the Degenerated are kept?"

Perrette nodded, "They're normally in the basement of the largest building, it's far enough away from the god to stop them affecting him." She caught his look, "Just because he's taken them on doesn't mean that they don't affect him or that they wouldn't cut him off given a chance."

"But if they kill him then they die."

"I don't think they can think that far."

"Do many of the gods have them?"

"I've heard some are starting to collect them," she admitted.

"Don't tell me, everyone wants to feel safe, even the gods."

"That's not Chris' fault. He's only ramped things up over the years."

"Why?" They were coming into the glade.

"I think he's jealous. The look on his face when he found out how old I was, he kept asking questions. He knows he can't go to another god, he'd end up as a Degenerated."

"So he feels hard done by."

"He's at that age where he knows he's not young anymore and he knows that a god might give out further favours if he proves useful."

"Didn't you tell him that most men have an affair with a much younger woman or buy an inappropriate car when they have a mid-life crisis? Fucking hell, doesn't he realise it's not all it's cracked up to be?"

Perrette's voice was soft, "He doesn't see it that way."

They stopped, all was still in the god's glade, very few people were there. "Where is everyone?"

"I sent them away little death worshipper. I would prefer them not to die." The god was stood by his pool.

"I don't kill people if they're minding their own business."

He smiled, "What about all those you killed at your friend's house. That boy by the way marker, you did nothing to help him. The scum in the alleyways or were they not worthy?"

He carried on and Tomas' breath became shorter at the relentless examples and he repeated, "I don't kill unless I have to."

"Now there's a lie. I think you secretly enjoy the fact that you can't survive without killing otherwise you'd allow yourself to die."

Tomas' fingers clenched the staff, "I try to kill as little as possible. Any life wants to keep living."

"Indeed and we gods share this wish also. This is why the larger prey on the smaller. Resources are not infinite you know."

"Not when you lead innocents to their death. The Degenerated, how many of those were people…"

The god interrupted, “Like yourself? With no knowledge of what they were doing?”

Tomas stared at his clenched hands, his knuckles were white. He couldn’t justify this argument, he could barely justify his own taking of life, only that he mourned every one. He didn’t do it for gain… he stopped himself. His own gain, to keep his life going. The childish sense that it wasn’t fair rose and he whispered it without realising.

“Life isn’t fair, but we can only try to make it so.” Perrette’s clear voice rang out across the glade as she answered his muttered words.

The god turned to her, “And that’s an interesting point from a worshipper of a god of mischief.”

“Well, you know how it is. Beggars can’t be choosers. Small gods don’t get the chance to pick the right candidate every time.”

The words cleared some of the mist from Tomas’ head. The god was trying to confuse him again. He stared hard as Perrette continued the battle of words, ignoring what she was saying. Dar had told Perrette to kill him, that he was dangerous. He’d been frightened, why? Tomas opened the channel between him and Al-Kiron, she was ready and waiting.

He ignored Perrette still fencing verbally and walked towards the pool and the statue, could he do this? Part of him was tense, he broke into a run. A hubbub of noise from the god and he swung the staff, the black blade appearing at the end, towards the statue.

It cut through the marble smoothly, toppling the figure onto the grass. He saw it crumble, the head rolling. The world shook, the buildings flickering and the trees swaying in a non-existent storm. Something howled, he peered through the tremor, his brain rattling and saw something inhuman where the god had been. Transparent it flailed, attempting to grasp the edges of reality. A shock of energy pierced him like an arrow and went through to Al-Kiron. She received it greedily and part of him felt another building going up in her glade. His legs gave way and he fell to the floor, seeing Perrette do the same.

The glade steadied, mist streaming towards the standing stone and spreading towards the plinth where the statue had stood. It twisted and solidified. Tomas groaned as another statue appeared, the same figure as had been there previously. Would he have to kill all the worshippers after all?

The glade returned to its former quiet. Tomas panted, feeling his brain settling back into a more human normality again. There were several buildings missing, he noticed the one Perrette had pointed out as housing the Degenerated was one of them. A dark moon was in the pool.

"May I ask what you intend to do now?" The god walked out from the shadow of the standing stone. This time he had a wariness about him.

Tomas pulled himself up. "That was a warning. I don't care what bargains you strike between you and your worshippers but no more pulling people into the Corridor with the intention of turning them into Degenerated."

"How will you enforce this ban?"

He took a gamble, "Because next time I aim for the stone." The god took a step back, his face white. "It's a simple matter of needing a deterrent to make you behave. If no one else can bring you into line then I will." He'd never wanted this, he was a simple man wanting simple pleasures and a simple life.

"You are a peasant."

"I am your death." He could feel Al-Kiron rising above him in the expectation of blood, her wings spreading out behind him. Together they could take the

Hall. She could become great again and rule all others, no one could withstand them and death would walk the Corridor. He shuddered under her onslaught, the beating of drums.

"No!" He had the sense of the whole Hall watching, life balancing on a pivot point. "You will stay where you are, safe in the outer reaches where no one can find you. My lady, I am grateful for what you have given me despite never wanting it. I would have been content to worship you as a simple potter and to have died as one but you will not use me in this way."

Tomas raised his head to stare at the god in his grove, "You call yourselves gods. You can give certain powers to those in the real world if you're willing to give up a large amount of yourselves but not many of you will do that. You're pretty powerless apart from the ability to confuse us once we're here." He took a deep breath, "I'm not going to justify what I do to live but you will behave otherwise you will find out the consequences. Where are Chris and Stef?"

The god bowed his head and made a strange gesture. "I have cut Chris off, his fate is in your hands now, I will have nothing more to do with him."

"You've made him a Degenerated?" Horror ran through Tomas, after all he'd said was he actually going to have to attempt to kill this god? For all his words, he didn't know what would happen if he swung his staff at the stone.

The god took a step away, "No, he is in your world. By cutting him off there, he can no longer reach the Hall."

"And Stef?"

"He was with Chris. Ask your own god to find him, he is hers not mine." He took a further step away into the shadow of the stone and disappeared. The moon faded from the pool and Tomas' legs collapsed underneath him.

Chapter 23

"What the fuck?" He could feel waves of exhaustion beating at him and couldn't work out why. Tomas hauled himself up onto his knees, feeling in a worse state than when he'd been an old man.

Perrette ran over to help him up, "We've spent too long here. I've got to get you to a way marker." She wriggled her head under his arm to brace him as he clung to the staff. "It's not far and there won't be any cribbet around or gaps in the landscape as it's well used round here."

"Let's hope we're not ambushed on the way."

"Only one way to find out Mr Doom and Gloom."

She helped him along the track until they came to the Corridor and they stopped at the people gathered there in silence. Tomas pulled himself away from her to stand on his own. He didn't think he could kill this many people, the Degenerated had been different, those herding them had been different. Even those he'd killed to maintain himself had not been the same. He flipped his hood down and stared at them.

"Well?" His quiet question challenged them and they parted to leave a path between them, leading down the Corridor.

"That's the way to the marker," whispered Perrette, she tucked her hand into his elbow.

Tomas nodded shortly and began walking. The dead silence was unnerving. No one's expressions were hostile, he kept his head up and nodded pleasantly to those watching him walk. There was no way he could walk faster, his exhaustion stopped that. The path slowly filled up behind them.

Close to the end, someone asked, "You're going to kill the Degenerated?"

Tomas stopped to find the speaker in the crowd and met his eyes. "Yes," he said simply.

Another asked, "You're going to keep the gods in check?"

He turned, not being able to pick this person out. "I think that's for all of us to do. Yes, they give us the power to get ourselves here but once we are, then their main ability is to confuse us until we capitulate." He shrugged, "So don't let them."

"They'll cut us off and make us into Degenerated."

"Then I'll have something to say about that. Up to that point it's up to you, I can't do this on my own." He began walking towards the way marker track. "I need to get out of here. I will come back shortly but I'm tired and I need to find my friend." Perrette's fingers were digging into his arm.

A murmur began to rise through the crowd. He had to stop himself from reacting to the implied danger until he realised people were talking, debating and arm waving, the noise growing. They swung onto the track and nearly walked into the slender man waiting for them.

"Well done, you only needed a little nudge in the end." Dar tucked his hand under Tomas' other arm and helped walk him a little faster.

"You mean you planned all this? You bastard…" Tomas made to swing at him and nearly fell over.

"You need to get back into your own world death worshipper, you're no good to anyone dead. Perrette, take him through and look after him."

"Why?" He could barely get his words out.

Dar let go as they came up to the marker stone. "I always like an outsider in the race, adds a bit of spice to the game." He laughed at Tomas' face and slid into the shadows.

Tomas was still cursing as they made the transfer. "That bastard…"

Perrette shoved him up against the wall and he wondered if there was a pleasanter way of being propped up. He almost smiled as she said, "That bastard still happens to be my god if you don't mind. I brought us back here as I couldn't think of where else to go. We need to get inside and eat, that'll help with the tiredness."

They were in Stef's back yard, the metal chairs and table had been shoved to one side and the gate bolted. Tomas could see the scars on the door from where the police had forced entry. A new lock had been put on amid the remains of the security tape.

"How do we get in?" Tomas sprawled onto a metal chair and indicated the door. "My key's not going to work in that."

Perrette waved a couple of slender lock picks. "This is my speciality – remember?" Within minutes she'd picked the lock and was helping him in. "Right, I know Stef keeps soup in the cupboard and bread in the freezer. He tends to work late and then forgets about eating until he's starving." At his querying look, she said, "He jokes about it a lot."

It felt a weird normality to be heating up soup and toasting bread with Perrette in someone else's kitchen. The smell alone made Tomas feel better, he doffed the cloak and leant the staff in the corner of the kitchen. Moppet was sprawled out asleep in the corner of the hall, he left her there. Perrette tossed her jacket over a chair and he found himself watching her slim figure in the small space and wondered if Stef had a spare bedroom.

Perrette caught his eye and smiled at him, pointedly turning her back to stir the pan. He roused himself to slide his arms around her, cupping her breasts and bending to kiss her neck. She stretched against him, sighing. His hunger switched from food to something a little more urgent.

"Couldn't switch that off for a moment could you?" He pulled her shirt out of her jeans, wanting to feel her bare skin and kissing harder. Perrette ignored his request, taking his hands to run them over herself and sliding them between her legs. He could feel her breath coming shorter, fuck the bedroom, this was happening now. Tomas undid his own jeans and pulled hers down. Her shaking was coming harder and he held off, determined to let her finish and pressed himself against her bare backside, winding himself up further.

The small noise was out of place, his fingers slowed and stopped. Perrette turned frowning, her mouth open to ask what the matter was and her question silenced by the look on his face. Tomas pulled his own trousers back up, raking his gaze over everything in the room, trying to work out what the matter was.

Something was pinging his senses that wasn't right. His eyes fell on a pan in the sink that hadn't been there before, crumbs were on the side in a different place to where they'd cut bread. Perrette turned the soup off, tucking herself in. A knife appeared in her hand. Tomas raised a finger to his lips and was caught by the puddle of fur sprawled out in the corner again. He stared, waiting for its ribs to move. Moppet had run under the chair when the men had burst in, he was sure she'd stayed out of the way. No breath stirred. He walked over on quiet feet and bent to touch her and found her cold.

He swore to himself, they'd not checked the rest of the house before they'd started messing around, a serious oversight, he'd been in this soft country too long. Perrette slid past him to check the front room and she came out shaking her head. That left upstairs. He reached out to his god and asked the question. She didn't answer, staying small and he noticed the drawer in the hall table was slightly ajar.

Perrette raised an eyebrow as he indicated upstairs. Those stairs were going to creak, whoever was up there would have a warning of them coming up. Tomas shrugged, took a deep breath and barrelled up them two at a time, Perrette behind him. He slammed the first two doors open, showing the empty bathroom and the bedroom. The third was locked. It gave to his shoulder and he stumbled in, trying to stop himself from falling over.

There were two people sat on chairs by the window, Stef had a black eye and his hands were cuffed together. His shirt was torn and he looked exhausted. Another set of hand cuffs attached him to a tall man with dark hair. Two mugs sat on the bedside table, soup stains on the rim. Tomas focussed on the gun held in Chris' hand. It was on his lap, he held it negligently pointing at Stef but Tomas had no doubt he could tighten his grip and fire within a second. It was the look in his eyes that made him go cold more than the gun, they were empty and hopeless.

"Chris." Perrette's voice was flat.

"Hello Perri, decided your freedom's too much for you?" Chris had no emotion left in his voice, this might have been a normal conversation. "Our friend led us a merry dance around the Corridor, he did well for someone with such little experience unfortunately he didn't know about building up tolerance to the place. We found him unconscious on a track. Aren't you pleased I rescued him and didn't leave him to the cribbet?"

Tomas bit down the reply that if it hadn't been for him them Stef would never have been in the Corridor.

"You had him hunting for me, that makes it even doesn't it?"

"Ah yes, the elusive Tomas. You were one on our lists that we weren't sure of. They recruited me in the hopes I might flush you out, and I recruited Stef." He smiled almost fondly at the other man. Stef remained slouched in the chair, not appearing to notice their conversation.

"And you found me." Tomas kept his voice light, trying not to look at the gun in Chris' lap.

"I found more than I ever thought was possible. Not only did you have long life but you have the ability to kill by touch. I couldn't believe your god refused to help you in that bar, not after I'd threatened you. I thought she would have transferred you to the Hall for safety."

"You threatened me?"

"I was the one shooting outside the bar," he shrugged. "Perri had confirmed you were making your way to the door."

Tomas struggled to contain his anger, innocent people had died so this man could flush him out. "You transferred to the Corridor after shooting, that's why there wasn't any evidence of the gun man, not even to your colleagues who were looking for you."

"Of course, you know now that modern technology drops into the void when we transfer. It can be useful. I flipped over to the toilets in the bar to watch. I can't believe that Al-Kiron hadn't brought you over before." Chris leaned forwards, his face still empty.

"Well you certainly made her do that in the bunker."

"I didn't anticipate the munitions pile exploding but thought having someone to protect might make you transfer. I had hoped you'd go to your god after you went through, you'd already confirmed what you could do in your flat with that recording of my underling dying. It was most fascinating to watch. Stop moving."

Tomas froze in his casual movements at the edge to Chris' voice. Perrette might be able to make the gun misfire, but he still needed to get to Chris to touch him. He didn't know if he could do it from a distance like in the Hall.

"You've only a minor god, she had you as a single follower for centuries and yet she gave you so much. My god could have given me more, so much more." Chris' eyes sparked and Tomas saw the embers flare under the emptiness. "He gave me the ability to know when someone uses their talent, Perri stopped the gun in the bar from actually killing you didn't she?"

Perrette didn't answer, her face was white in the doorway, she'd not moved while Chris had been talking and Tomas wondered if she could. Al-Kiron had refused to help him at the bar and he remembered the glacial stopping of pain in the hospital to get him out, the creep so slow it could barely be detected. She'd known Chris was around.

"You made her rig the odds of your man getting sepsis didn't you? Stef told me the machine failed as well."

"Of course, I couldn't have him talking could I? Perri told me all about you afterwards, it was a suitable punishment, don't you think darling?" Perrette dropped her head, her hair falling over her face. Tomas could see the hand holding the knife shaking. "All those years we were looking for you and we had someone in our midst who suspected who you were."

"You threatened Dar." Her whisper was tiny.

"Of course, we have ways of making you behave. Now, I have several bullets in this gun and I intend to use them. You're not in favour with the gods Tomas, they'd rather you weren't a bother to them. It's an easy solution to their problem." He cocked the gun and pointed it at Tomas. "I can then look at being brought back into the fold so to speak."

He was mad, Tomas stared down at the black hole in front of him. Perrette was useless, she appeared to have gone back into a waking nightmare, staring at the floor and shaking. "You won't be able to get to the Hall if you shoot me."

"Of course I will. "His voice was calm and reasonable, "Perri will take me, won't you dear." He appeared not to notice Perrette's distress. "I'll take Stef along as well and cuff him to a tree somewhere, he won't last long in the state he's in. It'll be a kindness."

Stef was still staring into nothing, Perrette was in a state, Tomas felt as though in a dream as Chris raised his arm and pointed the gun at him. This man had lost everything and yet he was still determined to take them with him, he couldn't understand why. The barrel of the gun looked huge as it was aimed at him, he couldn't move. He'd never felt this way, never in all his years had he faced anyone quite so nerveless.

Chris' finger tightened on the trigger and the gun clicked. Both of them focussed on the gun, not able to see what had happened. Then everything happened at once, Perrette threw herself at Chris, her face murderous and her knife raised ready. Stef shifted, grabbing for Chris' arm, pulled him sideways and they both disappeared.

Perrette staggered as she fell into the empty chairs, her face contorted. She was hissing to herself and Tomas reached out to touch her arm. She whirled, ready to slash again and he raised his hands, unnerved by the wildness in her eyes.

"Perrette, it's me, Tomas."

Her voice was low, "I'm going to carve that bastard's guts out."

"Put the knife down."

"You need to follow him, take me there."

"You can get to the Hall yourself, you don't need…"

Her voice was almost a scream, "Follow Stef you fucking idiot!"

"Perrette, please put that knife down." Tomas was only too aware that she could flip another one out of thin air should she choose to.

"Take me." She levelled the knife at him.

"Not while you have the knife Perrette." He took a careful step closer, attempting to stay as unthreatening as he could. He slid onto Stef's seat and held his hands out. "Please Perrette. Put it down."

"You don't know what he did to me…"

"We need to help Stef, I need to know I can trust you." The point was wavering, he reached out, his fingers gentle. Tomas pulled her into his arms as she dropped the knife and she buried her head into his shoulder, sobbing. Tomas rocked her while she cried, not expecting an explanation.

Eventually Perrette raised her head, her face wet and blotchy, "Why didn't you let me kill him?"

"Because I don't want you to." Tomas brushed a lock of hair out of her face. "Call it a stupid male thing but I don't like to see women killing. I've seen too much of it over the years." All that time spent in conflicts, the weak and vulnerable were always taken advantage of and when they had the chance to take revenge, the consequences were horrific. Normal law abiding women pushed to the limits would wreak injuries far worse than many men. Tomas held her tight, "Please tell me you won't."

"Bastard."

Tomas relaxed, the word held no heat and he asked, "Shall we go after Stef?" Perrette pushed herself away, nodding. He pulled them both up and concentrated, asking his god nicely to put them where Stef had gone. He was sure she was sulking after his refusal earlier. He reminded her that Stef was also her follower and he'd die if anything happened to him. Reluctantly she agreed and pulled them through.

A weariness hit him and his knees sagged again on arrival.

"We didn't eat and it doesn't help not having rested. We need to find Stef as soon as possible and get us all out of here." Perrette took a step and swore as her foot sank. "I can't believe Stef brought him through to here."

Tomas grabbed for her and pointed at the marks on the grass. "Looks like they not only came through but they fought as well." They carefully moved from tussock to grassy hump until they reached the path. Skid marks of mud showed the passage of the struggling men. The hoots and screeches of the unnatural woods made them both shiver.

"How far down are we?"

"I've no idea. Given the state of that way marker, probably quite a way."

They hurried the best they could along the track and saw a figure on the Corridor awkwardly carrying another in the distance.

"Stef!"

Stef turned, his face grey with exhaustion and his clothes torn. "Thank fuck you got here. I was wondering how I'd separate us. He told me he'd thrown the key into the void on the way back. I didn't want to move too far in case you didn't find me." He slung the still figure onto the ground. "Can you unpick them Perrette?"

"What are you going to do with him?" Her face was still.

Stef's eyes were hard, "I'm going to give him what he wants, the chance to become the only worshipper of a minor god. There are several entrances around here, I intend to leave him close by one or two."

Perrette breathed, "Around here the god might not have enough to send him back into the world."

"He might get eaten by something as well. Not my problem."

Her grin was vicious, "I'll undo the cuffs."

Tomas stared at them both in horror, "You two are revolting." It was the only thing he could think of saying.

"He deserves it." Perrette had her lock picks out and freed Stef in a few seconds. Stef clicked them back around Chris' wrists.

"Yes, he does." Stef threw him over his shoulder and walked in an easier manner up the Corridor to where two stones were almost opposite each other. He considered the space carefully while Tomas watched, the hair standing up on the back of his neck, and laid Chris down on the track.

Stef smacked the prone man lightly. "Wakey wakey," he said and walked away.

Epilogue

"I stole someone's bow while I was giving Chris the run around. I fancied myself as Hawkeye for a while – actually I'm not bad at it." Stef struck a pose, "Death on wings."

"Very funny." Tomas rolled his eyes as Perrette sniggered around her coffee cup. "So what actually happened, the first I knew people were shouting that there was a body in the toilets."

The outside café was in a busy side street, heaters giving it a continental feel and for once it wasn't raining. They were sat at one of the tables on the side, trying to keep their voices down. The number of people passing and talking felt reassuringly normal and safe.

"They followed me in. Have you any idea how difficult it is to do up your flies while someone's got their arm around your neck?" He shrugged, "I knew you'd come after me at some point and I was curious about the Corridor."

"You know that made you into a marked man."

"Well, I thought Chris might think that the other chap had brought me through and I was wandering about without being attached." Stef finished demolishing the huge cream cake he'd ordered with relish. "I wonder if one of those gods have won yet."

They'd seen Chris wake at a distance and watched his figure being pulled between the two gods. He'd lurched from side to side, staggering with his hands holding his head, neither of them strong enough to overcome the other. Stef had been watching with a certain satisfaction, Perrette had simply looked vicious.

Tomas shook his head, “Am I the only non-blood thirsty person here?”

“You’re a terrible advert for your god,” Perrette teased.

“Justice. You never know, one of them might get him.”

Tomas shuddered, he didn’t want to check. The pleading of a desperate god in your mind until you died wasn’t to be contemplated. He pushed his own plate away, no longer hungry and lit a cigarette. “You know, I can’t believe I didn’t die after killing all those Degenerated in the grove. She could have easily found another worshipper with everything I’d given her, several in fact.”

Perrette asked, “What would happen to everything she’d given you?”

“What do you mean? She’s been threatening me to make me behave for fucking centuries.”

“Yes but you’re linked in a way I’ve rarely seen. I don’t think she even dares to find out.”

Stef snorted, “She’s really played you one hasn’t she?”

“What?”

“You’ve threatened all the gods for her so they daren’t come after her and stopped her from having to move closer. She’s still back there, in the middle of nowhere where she can’t be found and she’s got a protector no one will dare come after.”

Perrette said, “Dar set this up as well, he was smirking when we left him despite you threatening him. It looks like certain gods have been trying to expand in different ways over the last century or so. It’s good to have a check on them.”

“Are you going to cull the Degenerated like you said?” Stef dragged Tomas’ discarded plate over and started demolishing the leftover cake.

"Yes. No one deserves that to happen to them."

"I found various buildings with them in, I'll help you." Stef looked at Perrette enquiringly.

She smiled at them both and pushed her chair back, "Not me. I've spent too long under someone else's thumb – I'm going to worship my god the way he intended me to." She cracked her knuckles in delight, "Look out for me."

"Will I see you again?" Tomas couldn't believe she was getting ready to leave.

Perrette grinned, "Maybe."

Tomas dropped his cigarette into the saucer and stood with her. They moved away from Stef and into the street. He was desperate to put his arms around her, she couldn't leave him, not now he'd found her. He tried, "You owe me a chance to make love to you properly. Candles and a meal, you in a dress."

"You were the one rushing last time – remember?"

"I rushed you? You couldn't keep your hands off me. What can I do to make you stay?"

"Nothing," Perrette laughed and then sobered. "You're not like Chris, you'll let me go."

"How can you tell?"

"All those times you watched me, just for a glimpse and then you left me to live my life. You're a romantic Tomas, keep looking and I'll see you around." She blew a kiss and slid into the crowd, her tall figure weaving in and out until she disappeared around the corner. Staring until he was jostled by someone, Tomas sat down and picked up his cigarette in a foul mood.

"She'll be back."

He didn't want to talk about it. All those years and she didn't want to stay. "She doesn't love me."

"She doesn't want to stay with you – that's different and it's fine. She'll pop back in touch when she wants to." Tomas glared at Stef and he simpered back, "Never mind – you've always got me."

"Fuck off."

The simper turned into laughter. "She likes you."

"Like hell."

"What does a woman have to do to prove she likes you? She stuck around to help fight all that shit away from your god. Yours and not hers, I might add. She didn't tell on you all those years - she likes you."

Tomas ground out the cigarette despite not having finished it and changed the subject. "I need to leave, get some paperwork sorted to make myself legit again."

"I've got shady contacts all over, I can get anything either of us need." He smiled, "I have favours I can pull in to help."

"Hang on, you don't need to disappear."

"Actually I think it'll be a good idea. While I've managed to sort out your records so you're no longer a wanted man, other people now know who I am. Both you and Al-Kiron could be found through me."

"I was going to head back to Europe, I have papers I can use there. You might be a problem though."

"My mother was Flemish. I can speak fluent French, a bit of Dutch and I can swear proficiently in German. I'm not so useless."

Tomas thought things through slowly, it would be nice to have company after so many years alone and smiled at the thought of travelling with Stef. "Get your stuff ready but don't disappear from your life here yet, you might find it more troublesome than you think."

"What are you going to do?"

"When I've got a stable identity again, I can look at dealing with the Degenerated and decided how I'm going to keep these so called gods in line. Fancy helping?"

Stef's grin was all he needed and Tomas laughed, feeling lighter than he had for a long time. For the first time in centuries he had a friend who knew what he was, he had the chance to find out more about the strange beings inhabiting the Hall and Perrette would come back when she was ready - she knew where Al-Kiron was and his god owed her a favour for helping.

Life was there for the taking.

***

www.ingramcontent.com/pod-product-compliance
Lightning Source LLC
LaVergne TN
LVHW010055170826
845678LV00012B/2148

* 9 7 8 1 8 3 8 2 1 5 7 8 1 *